THE WILD THINGS
BY DAVE EGGERS

Seven-year-old Max likes to make noise, get dirty, ride his bike with-out a helmet and howl like a wolf. In any other era, he would be considered a boy. In 2007, he is considered wilful and deranged. His home life is problematic. His parents are divorced; his father, immature and romantic, lives in the city. His mother has taken up with a younger man who steals quarters from the change bowl in the foyer. Driven by a series of pressures, internal and external, Max leaves home, jumps in a boat and sails across the ocean to a strange island where giant beasts reign – the Wild Things from Maurice Sendak's visionary classic.

This is an all-ages adventure, full of wit and soul, that explores the chaos of youth while Max explores the chaos of the world around him.

Dave Eggers is the author of *A Heartbreaking Work of Staggering Genius*, *You Shall Know Our Velocity*, *How We Are Hungry*, *What is the What* and the forthcoming *Zeitoun*. He is also the co-writer, with Spike Jonze, of the live-action film *Where the Wild Things Are*, directed by Jonze and released in late 2009.

THE WILD THINGS
A NOVEL BY DAVE EGGERS

ADAPTED FROM THE ILLUSTRATED BOOK
WHERE THE WILD THINGS ARE
by

MAURICE SENDAK

AND BASED ON THE SCREENPLAY
WHERE THE WILD THINGS ARE
co-written by DE and

SPIKE JONZE

HAMISH HAMILTON
an imprint of
PENGUIN BOOKS

HAMISH HAMILTON

Published by the Penguin Group
Penguin Books Ltd, 80 Strand, London WC2R 0RL, England
Penguin Group (USA) Inc., 375 Hudson Street, New York, New York 10014, USA
Penguin Group (Canada), 90 Eglinton Avenue East, Suite 700, Toronto, Ontario, Canada M4P 2Y3
(a division of Pearson Penguin Canada Inc.)
Penguin Ireland, 25 St Stephen's Green, Dublin 2, Ireland (a division of Penguin Books Ltd)
Penguin Group (Australia), 250 Camberwell Road,
Camberwell, Victoria 3124, Australia (a division of Pearson Australia Group Pty Ltd)
Penguin Books India Pvt Ltd, 11 Community Centre, Panchsheel Park, New Delhi – 110 017, India
Penguin Group (NZ), 67 Apollo Drive, Rosedale, North Shore 0632, New Zealand
(a division of Pearson New Zealand Ltd)
Penguin Books (South Africa) (Pty) Ltd, 24 Sturdee Avenue, Rosebank, Johannesburg 2196, South Africa

Penguin Books Ltd, Registered Offices: 80 Strand, London WC2R 0RL, England

www.penguin.com

First published in the United States of America by McSweeney's 2009
First published in Great Britain by Hamish Hamilton 2009
1

For more information about McSweeney's: www.mcsweeneys.net

Printed in Great Britain by Clays Ltd, St Ives plc

A CIP catalogue record for this book is available from the British Library

ISBN: 978–0–241–14455–8

www.greenpenguin.co.uk

For Maurice Sendak, an unspeakably brave and beautiful man

CHAPTER I

Matching Stumpy pant for pant, Max chased his cloud-white dog through the upstairs hallway, down the wooden stairs, and into the cold open foyer. Max and Stumpy did this often, running and wrestling through the house, though Max's mother and sister, the two other occupants of the home, didn't appreciate the volume and violence of the game. Max's dad lived in the city and phoned on Wednesdays and Sundays but sometimes did not.

Max lunged toward Stumpy, missed, barreled into the front door, and knocked the doorknob-basket off. The doorknob-basket was a small wicker vessel that Max thought was stupid but Max's mom insisted on having on the front doorknob for good luck. The main thing the basket was good for was getting knocked off, and landing on the floor, where it was often stepped on. So Max knocked the basket off, and then Stumpy stepped on it, putting his foot through the bottom with an unfortunate wicker-ripping sound. Max was worried for a second, but then his worry was eclipsed by the sight of Stumpy trying to walk around the house with a basket stuck to his foot. Max laughed and laughed. Any reasonable person would see the humor in it.

"Are you going to be a freak all day?" Claire asked, suddenly standing over Max. "You've only been home for ten minutes."

His sister Claire was fourteen, almost fifteen, and was no longer interested in Max, not on a consistent basis at least. Claire was a freshman now and the things they always liked to do together — including Wolf and Master, a game Max still thought worthy — were no longer so appealing to her. She had adopted a tone of perpetual dissatisfaction and annoyance with everything Max did, and with most things that existed in the world.

Max didn't answer Claire's question; any response would be problematic. If he said "No," then it would imply he had been acting freakish, and if he said "Yes," it would mean that not only had he been a freak, and he was admitting it, but that he intended to *continue* being a freak.

"You better make yourself scarce," Claire said, repeating one of their dad's favorite expressions. "I'm having people over."

If Claire had been thinking clearly, she would have known that to tell Max to become *scarce* would only make him want to be *more prominent*, and to tell him that she was having people over would only make him more committed to being present. "Is Meika coming?" he asked. Meika was his favorite among Claire's friends, the rest of whom were imbeciles. Meika paid attention to him, actually talked to him, asked him questions, had one time even come into his room to play Lego and admire the wolf suit he kept on his closet door. She had not forgotten what was fun.

"None of your business," Claire said. "Just leave us alone, okay? Don't ask them to play with your blocks or whatever lame crap you want them to do."

Max knew that watching and annoying Claire and her friends would be better with someone else, so he went outside, got on his bike, and rode down the street to Clay's. Clay was a new kid; he lived in one of the just-built houses down the street. And though he was pale and his head too big, Max was giving him a chance.

Max rode down the sidewalk serpentine-style, his head full of possibilities for what he and Clay might do with or, barring that, *to* Claire's friends. It was December and the snow, dry and powdery just a few days earlier, was now melting, leaving slush on the roads and sidewalks, a patchy cover on the lawns.

Something was happening in Max's neighborhood. The old houses were being taken down, and in their place, new, bigger and louder houses were rising. There were fourteen homes on his block, and in the last two years, six of them, all of them smallish, one-story ranches, had been leveled. In each case the same thing had happened: the owners had left or had died of old age, and the new owners had decided that they liked the location of the house, but wanted a far larger one where it stood. It brought to the neighborhood the constant sound of construction, and, thankfully for Max, a near-endless supply of castoff materials — nails, wood, wire, insulation, and tile. With it all he'd been assembling a sort-of home of his own, in a tree, in the woods by the lake.

Max pedaled up, dropped his bike, and knocked on the door of Clay Mahoney. He bent down to tie his shoes, and as he finished the second knot on his left shoe, the door flew open.

"Max?" Clay's mother stood over him, wearing tight black pants and a small white T-shirt — TODAY! YES! it said — over a black lycra top; she was dressed like a competitive downhill skier. Behind her, an exercise video had been paused on the television. On the screen, three muscular women were reaching upward and rightward, desperate and grimacing, for something far beyond the frame.

"Is Clay home?" Max asked, standing up.

"No, I'm sorry Max, he's not."

She was holding a large, silver canister with a black handle — some sort of coffee mug — and while taking a sip from it, she looked around the front porch.

"Are you here alone?" she asked.

Max thought a second about this question, looking for a second meaning. Of course he was here alone.

"Yup," he said.

She had a face, Max had noticed, that always seemed surprised. Her posture and voice aimed at knowingness, but her eyes said *Really? What? How is that possible?*

"How'd you get here?" she asked.

Another odd question. Max's bike was lying no more than four feet behind him, in plain sight. Could she not see it?

"I rode," he said, jerking a thumb over his shoulder.

"Alone?" she asked.

"Yup," he said. *This lady*, Max thought.

"Alone?" she repeated. Her eyes had gone wide. Poor Clay. His mom was nuts. Max knew he should be careful about what he might say to a crazy person. Didn't crazy people need to be treated with great care? He decided to be very polite.

"Yes, Mrs. Mahoney. I… am… alone." He said the words slowly, carefully, maintaining eye contact all the while.

"Your parents let you ride around on your own? In December? Without a helmet?"

This lady definitely had a problem grasping the obvious. It was obvious that Max was alone, and obvious that he had ridden his bike. And there was nothing on his head, so why ask about the helmet? She was delusional on top of it all. Or maybe functionally blind?

"Yes, Mrs. Mahoney. I don't need a helmet. I live just down the block. I rode here on the sidewalk."

He pointed down the street to his own house, which was visible from her door. Mrs. Mahoney put her hand on her forehead and squinted, like a castaway searching the horizon for a rescue vessel. She dropped her hand, returned her eyes to Max, and sighed.

"Well, Clay is at his quilting class," she said. Max didn't know what a quilting class was, but it sounded a lot less fun than making icicle-spears and throwing them at birds, which had been on Max's mind.

"Well, okay. Thanks, Mrs. Mahoney. Tell him I came by," he said. He waved goodbye to Clay's crazy mom, turned, and got on his bike. He heard the Mahoney's door shut as he coasted away. But when he turned onto the sidewalk and toward his house, he found Mrs. Mahoney next to him, striding purposefully, still holding her silver drink canister.

"I can't let you go alone," she said, striding briskly alongside him.

"Thanks, Mrs. Mahoney, but I ride alone every day," he said, pedaling cautiously and again maintaining steady eye contact. Her weirdness had tripled and his heartbeat had doubled.

"Not today you don't," she said, grabbing for the seat of Max's bike.

Now he was getting scared. This woman was not only nuts, but she was following him, grabbing at him. He picked up speed. He figured he could ride faster than she could walk, and he intended to do so. He was now standing on his pedals.

She picked up her pace — still walking! Her elbows were flying left and right, her mouth a quick slash of determination. Was she smiling?

"Ha!" she giggled. "Fun!"

It was always the nuttiest people who smiled while doing the nuttiest things. This lady was far gone.

"Please," he said, now pedaling as fast as he possibly could. He almost hit a mailbox, the Chungs', the one bearing a large peace sign; this had caused great controversy in the neighborhood. "Just let me go," he begged.

"Don't worry," she huffed, now at a full jog. "I'll be right here the whole way."

How could he shake her? Would she follow him inside his own house? She was no doubt waiting to get him alone and indoors, so she could do something to him. She could knock him cold with the coffee canister. Or maybe she'd grab a pillow, pin him down, and suffocate him? That seemed more her style. She had the clear-eyed, efficient look of a murderous nurse.

Now there was barking. Max turned to see that the Scolas' dog had joined them, barking at Mrs. Mahoney and nipping her ankles. Mrs. Mahoney took little notice. Her eyes were bigger than ever. The exertion seemed to make her ever-more gleeful.

"Endorphins!" she sang. "Thanks, Max!"

"Please," he said. "What are you gonna do to me?" It was about ten houses until his own.

"Keep you safe," she said, "from all this."

She waved her arm around, indicating the neighborhood that Max was born into and in which he'd been raised. It was a quiet street of tall elms and oaks, ending in a cul-de-sac. Beyond the cul-de-sac was a wooded few acres, then the lake. Nothing nefarious or of note had ever happened on this street, or in their town, or, for that matter, within four hundred miles.

Max swerved suddenly, leaving the sidewalk. He jumped the curb into the road.

"The road!" Mrs. Mahoney gasped, as if he'd steered his bike into a river of molten lava. The road was empty now and was always empty. But soon she was right behind him, now running, again reaching for his seat.

Max decided it was silly to go home; that's where she

wanted him. He'd be trapped and she'd finish him for sure. His only chance of escape would be the forest.

He sped up again, giving himself enough room to turn around. He did a quick 180 and headed back toward the dead-end, hoping to make it to the woods.

"Where are you going?" she wailed.

Max almost laughed. She wouldn't follow him into the woods, would she? He looked back, and though she'd lost a step or two, it wasn't long before she was sprinting at him. Man, she was fast! He was close to the road's end, almost at the trees.

"I won't let you out of my sight!" she falsettoed. "Don't worry!"

He jumped the curb again — eliciting a terrified howl from Mrs. Mahoney — and jumbled over the rough grass and snow. Soon he was quickly ducking under the first low branches of the tall white-mustached pines, weaving between the trunks.

"MAAAAAX!" she wailed. "Not the woods!"

He entered the forest and headed toward the ravine.

"Molesters! Drugs! Homeless! Needles!" she gasped.

The ravine was up ahead, about twenty feet deep and twelve feet wide. A month earlier, over the gap he'd put a wide bridge of plywood. If he could get to the gap, cross the bridge, and then pull the plank away in time, he might finally be free.

"Stop!" she yelled.

He swung his bike underneath him, left and right. He'd never ridden so fast. Even the Scola dog was having trouble keeping up; he was still yapping at the lady's heels.

"Look out!" she screamed. "The what-do-you-call-it! The gorge!"

Duh, he thought. He made it to the bridge and again came a howl of incalculable terror. "Nooooooo!"

He rumbled quickly over the plank. On the other side, he spun out, dropped his bike, and grabbed the plywood. She was almost upon him when he pulled the board free. The bridge fell into the ravine and crashed against the rocks below.

She stopped short. "Dammit!" she yelled. She stood for a second, hands on hips, heaving. "How do you expect me to protect you when you're all the way over there?"

Max thought of a few clever answers to this question, but instead said nothing. He mounted his bike again, in case Mrs. Mahoney decided to leap over the gap. She was far stronger and faster than he would have guessed, so he couldn't rule it out.

At that moment, the Scolas' dog, still running at full speed, chose to pass Mrs. Mahoney, jump over the ravine, and join Max. He flew, effortlessly, and landed on Max's side. He turned back to face her, then looked up to Max with a toothy grin and happy eyes, as if the two of them had together vanquished a common enemy. Max laughed, and when the dog began barking at the woman doubled over on the edge of the ravine, Max barked, too. They both barked and barked and barked.

CHAPTER II

"Hey Claire!" Max yelled into the house. No answer.

He couldn't wait to tell her about Mrs. Mahoney, that lunatic. Claire wasn't always interested in what Max was interested in, but she always liked stories about crazy people. This one was going to knock her flat.

"Anyone here?" he asked, hoping only for his sister. Gary, his mom's boyfriend with a chin as soft as cake, sometimes came over early after work and napped on the couch. He stained any room he spilled himself into.

"Claire?"

Max looked in the kitchen, the living room, the basement. No sign of Claire. He walked upstairs and finally heard her.

"I *didn't* show him. That's the *point*," she was saying.

She was on the phone when Max entered her room, the first words of his story about to leave his mouth. Before he could begin, though, she fixed him with a look of great venom. He tiptoed out quickly.

"But why would she *say* that? She's totally lying!"

He waited outside her door. When she was finished, he'd tell her all about Mrs. Mahoney, his triumph, and together they'd plan some kind of prank on the loony lady.

But then again, why wait? Max knew Claire would want to hear this right away, and would thank him — for saving her from that troublesome conversation and delivering her into a much better one — just as soon as she heard Max's tale. He walked back into her room and—

"Get out, goddammit!" she screamed.

He stood for a moment, so shocked he couldn't move or speak. This wasn't at all the way he'd pictured things happening.

"Get out!" she screamed again, twice as loud as before, and kicked the door closed in his face.

His rage was fathomless, and was directed, with all its awesome power, at Claire. What had he done? He'd walked into her room. He'd wanted to talk to her. It wasn't right or fair for her to treat him like she did, and she knew it.

And now she was going to pay the price.

There was still enough snow for effective construction, so he decided to carve a fort, state of the art, out of the snowbank across the street. And when her friends showed up, Max would be ready, and all would be avenged. It would be ugly, but she'd asked for it.

He put on his snow clothes and ran across the street. Using his mom's gardening trowel, he dug and dug into the snowmass, soon finishing the main inner chamber. It was big enough to fit him and maybe one other person his size, and with a roof high enough that he could sit up inside. With the trowel, he carved a long deep shelf in the inner wall of the cave, to hold snowballs and maybe food or books. If he could get an extension cord long and sturdy enough, he figured, he could set up a TV. But that would have to wait until later.

Into the wall facing his house he dug a narrow peep-hole. Now he had a perfect view of the driveway and the front door of his house. He would be ready when Claire's friends showed up and did their usual thing of standing in the driveway, talking and pretending to know how to chew tobacco and then spitting and drooling the brown juice into the grey snow.

Max looked at his watch, noting that it was 4:15, which meant that he probably had another fifteen minutes before they arrived. Claire's friends showed up — when they did show up, because sometimes they didn't, though they said they would — at 4:30 or so every day, because one of the boys who always came, bed-headed and called Finn, had to do after-school detention every day of the year. Who would pick a guy like that up from detention just to enjoy his company? Claire and her idiot friends. They all waited at school for the fumbler named Finn, then came to Max's house for some reason.

Max used the time to amass a vast arsenal. The snow was a perfect texture, just wet enough to be sticky. All he needed to do was grab a handful and it was already a snowball — snowballs that almost made themselves. Each one he would pack tight from all sides, smooth over, pack again, smooth over again, and then put on the shelf. In ten minutes he had packed thirty-one snowballs and had run out of room on his shelf.

So he built another shelf.

With the remaining five minutes, Max decided he needed a flag on top of his fort, so he left the cave and stood and searched around the surrounding woods for a stick, and found one about four feet tall and as straight as a flagpole. He stuck it into the roof of the fort and then tied his hat onto it. He backed up and was satisfied that it truly almost looked like a flag — a flag raised for a great nation and before a glorious and morally necessary battle.

At 4:30 he was back in the cool comfort of his fort, peering through the peephole, watching for any movement at his house. No, he wasn't cold. One might think that a boy who was out in the snow for so long would get cold, but Max was not. He was warm, partly because he had on many layers, and partly because boys who are part wolf and part wind do not get cold.

At 4:38, a station wagon pulled into his driveway. It was a car he knew well, an ancient red station wagon one of the boys who came around drove. Two boys and a girl got out. One boy was the bed-headed one named Finn. Another always wore black; this was Carlos. The girl was named Meika, and Max loved her without boundary.

Max could make out parts of a conversation as they walked into his house.

"Did Tonya tell you she didn't do it?" Meika said.

"Yeah, she did," Carlos said.

"That doesn't mean we believe her," Finn said.

The front door opened and Claire emerged.

"Speak of the devil," Carlos said.

"What?" Claire said, and they all laughed.

Claire pretended to laugh, too, and they all filed past her and into the house. A minute later they emerged again. They probably wanted to chew tobacco, and Claire knew not to allow it in the house; their mom could always tell, hours or days later. As the boys, and Claire, began their disgusting coughing and spitting, Max knew the stage was set. He knew what he had to do. "Okay. Okay," he said to himself. "Okay."

He snaked out of the fort's entrance, making sure he was undetected by the four targets across the street. Now standing across the street, he looked closely at Claire and her friends and confirmed that he had not been detected. He reached back into the fort for his ammunition. He gathered the snowballs carefully into all of his available pockets. When his pockets were full, he placed the rest kangaroo-style in the front of his coat. He left twenty snowballs in the fort, in case he needed to replenish his supply later.

Now he had to get closer. He needed to cross the street and position himself in the neighbor's yard. There, he would have a fence to protect himself from the enemy fire. But it was a long way across the street, and surely they would see him running no more than forty feet away.

Then he had an idea.

He took one of his smaller snowballs and threw it as far as he could. He could throw far — he could throw a baseball forty-four miles an hour, according to the radar thing at the batting cages — so the snowball, a small one, sailed over the heads of Claire and her friends and into the far-neighbor's yard. When it landed, it made a loud scratchy sound and the four teenagers all turned to see where the sound had come from. While they were distracted, Max darted across the street and dove behind the other neighbor's fence.

The plan worked. He was smarter than he could stand. He advanced quickly.

He was now only about twenty feet away from the enemy, with the neighbor's fence obscuring them. The four teenagers were doing their business with the chewing tobacco, the boys putting it in their mouths, the girls saying, "That stuff's nasty," and then saying other things that were stupid and were not worth saying. All the while, none of them had any idea that they were about to endure a devastating assault.

Max dropped all his snowballs onto the ground below him, and placed a line of ammunition on the lower beam of the fence. He kept seven snowballs in his various pockets, in case he needed to advance on the enemy and finish them off.

Finally he was ready. He took a long breath, heaving out something like dragon steam, and he began.

He unleashed a barrage of five snowballs, one after the other, throwing them faster than even he thought possible. His arm was some kind of machine, like a tennis-ball cannon.

Boom!

Boom!

Boom!

One hit the bed-headed kid in the chest. The sound was incredible, a hollow pop against his puffy jacket.

"What the hell?" he yelled.

Another smacked Meika in the thigh.

"Ah! What the!" she gasped.

One thumped onto the station wagon's windshield; again the sound was great. Two missed their targets completely but it didn't matter — Max was already unloading another barrage. Four more left his cannon-arm, and these hit Claire's shoulder, the car's roof and door, and Carlos, right in the groin. He doubled over. Fantastic.

"Who is that?" Claire yelled.

Max ducked behind the fence but not before the boys deduced that Max was the source of the assault. They had figured out his position. Max got another arsenal ready, but when he peeked over the fence again — "There's the little bastard!" one said — he was met by an avalanche of snow, which fell upon his head and back with great force and speed. The boys had been fast, and deposited a boulder of snow over the fence and onto Max. The fight was moving beyond artillery and into hand-to-hand combat sooner than Max had expected.

"How's that feel, wuss?"

"You hit me in the balls, idiot."

If Max could run across the street, he would be safe. Even if they followed him across the street, they would never be able to find his well-hidden fort, much less penetrate his defenses. He took off.

"Run, little grasshopper! Run!" they said.

"Look at his little legs go!"

As he began running, he launched one last snowball, arcing it so high it disappeared into the sun before Max could see where it would land.

He ran, and was across the street before the boys had even decided to follow. He zig-zagged through the pines to throw them off the scent, and then heard the last snowball land with an icy smack.

"Max, you freak!" he could hear Claire saying. "You hit Meika in the face!"

That was a shame, Meika was the one he hadn't wanted to hit at all. Maybe she would think him more muscular because he'd hit her in the face? Did it ever work that way? He thought maybe. Max grinned as he reached the entrance to the fort. Maybe Meika would kiss him and touch his neck because he hit her in the face with snow.

He looked out his peephole, and could see Claire helping Meika, who was crying, her face red and raw. Why would anyone cry about getting hit in the face with a ball of ice and snow falling from the sky after almost hitting the sun?

Max was disappointed in her. Girls were such girls. Pretty soon Meika would be crying all the time, about everything, which is what Max's mom seemed to do. A few years ago Max had said, "What's wrong?" and "Don't cry, Mom," but now there didn't seem to be a point.

"Where'd he go?" one of the boys said. Max could hear the voice, but couldn't find its source through his peephole.

"Wait. Check out the flag," said the other boy.

Max made a mental note: next time, no flag.

He heard the footsteps of the two boys very close to his fort. Man, they were fast. Now they were behind him. He turned around and could see their feet just beyond the entrance to the cave.

"He's in there," one said. "I can see his stupid boots."

"Hey kid, you in there?" the other asked.

"He's in there," the first said again. "The boots, dude."

"Come out, or we'll get you out."

Max was starting to worry. It really did seem like they knew where Max's fort was, and that he was inside it. He was stuck if he stayed in the fort, and would probably be slaughtered if he left it. His options seemed few.

Now a hand was inside the fort. One of the boys had shoved his arm through the roof. How'd he do that? Max kicked it, hard, and it retreated.

"Ow! Now you're dead, kid," a voice said.

Then it was very quiet for a moment.

And Max could no longer see their feet.

He heard some giggling, then some shushing.

Then it was quiet for a very long moment.

Now footsteps on the roof. A bit of snow-dust fell from the ceiling. Max felt safe, though, knowing that there were many layers of well-packed snow between the roof and his chamber. They stepped and stepped. So what, Max thought. Step all you want.

Then they jumped.

The sound was like a low, loud cough.

They jumped again.

More snowdust fell from the ceiling. The roof drew

closer to Max's head. He shrunk down, now laying flat. But still the ceiling seemed to be falling.

The crunch of earth swallowing earth.

They jumped once more.

Then white. All was white.

And the cold, the cold! It was in his jacket, in his eyes, his nose, his pants. He couldn't breathe. He could hear almost nothing. He was drowning.

Then he heard the laughing. The boys were laughing.

"Nice fort," one said.

"Come out," the other said.

Max couldn't move. He wasn't sure he was alive.

"Get up, little grasshopper," a voice said.

Max couldn't move. *Was* he alive?

"Oh crap," said a voice.

The sounds of digging. Furious scratching above.

The weight on Max's back lightened and he found himself being lifted out of the white. The boys were pulling him up, and soon he was in the air again, breathing the light air. But he had no strength. He couldn't stand. He fell to the ground like a puppet.

Laying on the snow, he coughed and coughed. His eyes were soaked, his skin scorched. His eyes didn't work, his mouth would not open. His lungs heaved, his throat burned.

"You okay?" one of them asked.

Max rose to his knees, but couldn't speak. He choked on snow and phlegm. His heart seemed to have split itself, migrated northward, and was now beating in each of his ears.

Where was Claire? She should have been with him by

now. Holding his shoulder. Rubbing his neck. Cupping her hands around his ears, blowing hotly to warm him as she did just a year ago, when he had fallen through the ice in the creek after the blizzard.

But Claire was not near. Max stood up and the snow in his jacket drained down his back. He shuddered and shook. He looked to his sister, but she was attending to Meika, and seemed ready to let Max, her brother, die in the middle of this colorless afternoon in December.

"You hurt, kid?" one of the boys said. The other one had already walked back to the car.

The horn honked. Now the second boy shrugged, left Max, and ran to it. Claire lingered on the driveway for a second, glancing Max's way. For that brief moment Max held out hope that she would come to him, that she would take him inside, draw him a bath, stay with him and curse the boys and never see them again. That she would be his sister again.

"Your brother's kind of sensitive, huh?" a face said from the car's open window. It was Finn, the wild-haired kid.

"You have no idea," Claire said. She turned away from Max, ducked into the back seat, and closed the door. The car backed out and drove off.

CHAPTER III

Max no longer had a sister.

He walked back to the house, and before he knew exactly what he was doing, he found himself in the kitchen, where he looked under the sink and retrieved a large pail. He turned the pail over, emptying it of its cleaners and sprays and brushes. He brought the pail upstairs, to the bathroom he shared with Claire.

He turned on the bathtub's faucet and placed the bucket below. As it filled with water, he caught a glimpse of himself in the bathroom mirror. He was soaked, every part of his body was wet, and his face was red, feral. He liked how he looked.

The bucket was full and he reached down to lift it. Too heavy, so he emptied the top third. He took the bucket, sloshing to and fro, and brought it to Claire's room.

It was a room in transition. She had always had a frilly bed of pink and powder blue, a canopy above, but now over the bed was an ugly crocheted blanket, something she had bought in the parking lot of some concert in the city.

Before he thought one way or the other about it, he dumped his bucket on her bed, where the water made a loud splash and instantly spread over the surface of the mattress.

He went back to the bathroom, where the faucet was still running. He filled the bucket again and returned to Claire's room, this time dumping the contents on the floor, where the carpet soaked up the water immediately. It was satisfying, but only whetted his appetite. He filled the bucket again and again and dumped its contents again and again, drenching her dresser, her closet — every part of her room. He emptied seven buckets this way, pouring water on the chair where she threw her clothes, on her closeted collection of dolls and animals and field hockey equipment, on the bulletin board where she had collaged pictures of herself and her worthless friends.

It was a very workmanlike process, getting the water and pouring it all over Claire's room, but Max felt that it had to be done. It was his job, at that moment, to pay Claire back for allowing him to be crushed under a hundred pounds of snow, and for ignoring him, for allowing her friends to nearly kill him. He was sure that this step, soaking her room, was the first of many on the way to the two of them no longer being siblings. She would probably want to move out so she could live with Meika or get married to one of the stoners and live on a farm in Vermont, which is what she was always talking about doing some day. She wanted her own farm, she said, where she could make ice cream and sell handmade dolls and the kind of bookmarks she'd recently learned to crochet.

That would be fine, Max thought. As long as she left, Max didn't care where she went. He just wanted her out of the house so he wouldn't have to have someone betray him like this ever again. He would live happily with his mom, especially after he got rid of her boyfriend, Gary, who Max didn't want to think about at that particular moment.

He stood for a moment on the soggy carpet, now dotted with small lakes. Calming down and surveying the damage, he began to have conflicting thoughts about what he had done.

CHAPTER IV

The coming night had colored his room an airless, cottony blue. From his lower bunk, he switched on both of his globes — antiques his father had bought him, from another time, each aglow from a light within. The bulbs resided deep inside, where the earth's liquid core would be, and gave the globes' oceans and continents a buttery tint.

Max lay in his bed and thought awhile.

His thoughts, he knew, sometimes behaved like the scattering birds of his neighborhood. Everywhere on Max's block were quail — strange, flop-topped birds reluctant to fly. One moment the quail would be assembled, in a straight row, a family, eating the seed from the ground, with one standing guard atop a low fencepost, watching for intruders. Then, with the slightest sound, they all would scatter in a dozen directions, swerving and disappearing into the thicket.

Every so often Max felt his thoughts could be straightened out, that they could be put in a row and counted; they could be made to behave. There were days when he could read and write for hours on end, when he understood everything said to him in every class, when he could eat dinner calmly and help clean up, and then play quietly alone in the living room.

But there were other times, other days, most days really, when the thoughts did not line up. Days when he chased the various memories and impulses as they veered and scattered away from him, hiding in the thicket of his mind.

And it seemed that when this happened, when he couldn't make sense of something, when the thoughts did not flow from one to the other, that on the heels of the scattering quail he did things and said things that he wished he had not said or done.

Max wondered why he was the way he was. He didn't want to hate Claire and he didn't want to have destroyed her room. He didn't want to have broken the window over the kitchen sink when he thought he was locked out of the house — which he'd done a few months ago. He didn't want to have screamed and pounded the walls of his room last year, when in the middle of the night he couldn't find the door. There were so many things he'd done, so many things he'd broken or torn or said, and always he knew he'd done them, but could only half-understand why.

And it occurred to him that he might be in real trouble. Until then it had seemed simple enough. He had almost died in the fort, so he soaked his sister's room and tore up any evidence of any affection he had ever had for her.

But now that simple plan, inevitable and logical, seemed less wise than it had only moments ago. His mom might not appreciate Max having thrown seven buckets of water into Claire's room. It was so strange to think about: how was it that just minutes ago, doing all that had seemed like the only thing to do? He hadn't even questioned it. It was the only idea in his head, and he carried it out with great speed and determination. Now he was listening to his mother's footsteps on the stairs, coming up to see him, and he felt like erasing the past, everything he had ever done. He wanted to say, *I know I've always been bad, and now I will be good. Just let me live.*

"Anyone home?" Max's mother asked. "Max?"

He could escape. He could slip downstairs and run out the front door. Could he? He could live in another town, he could hop trains, become a hobo. He could leave, try to explain himself in a note, wait it out while everyone calmed down. He was sure that there would be anger, and yelling and stomping, maybe that violent sort of silence his mother had perfected. He didn't want to be around for all that.

So he got ready to leave home for good.

He retrieved his backpack, the one his father had bought him before they hiked through Maine. But just as he was getting up to put on dry clothes and pack the bag, his mom was there, door open, already in his room, standing over him.

"What's happening in here? Anything good?" she asked.

She was wearing her work clothes, a wool skirt and

white cotton blouse. She smelled of cold air and sweat and something else. God, he loved her so much. She sat down on his bed and kissed his head. He briefly fell apart, disintegrated by her gentle touch. But then he placed the smell: it was Gary's deodorant, which she had begun sharing. It was a wet, chemical smell.

He sat back in his bed and his eyes welled. How could so many tears come so quickly? Stupid crying. So stupid. He threw the covers over his face.

"What's wrong?" she asked.

Max didn't answer. He couldn't look at her.

"Are you mad at me?" she asked.

Max was surprised by this question, though it wasn't a new one. For a second, it gave him strength. It reminded him there were other problems, other people to blame.

"No," he said.

She pulled the covers down from his face.

"What is it then?" she asked. "Were you crying?"

"Claire's stupid friends smashed my igloo," he said. It came out far sooner than he'd planned.

"Oh," his mom said, running her hand through his matted hair. She didn't seem very impressed with the crime. He knew he had to make his mom furious at what Claire had done. If he made her angry enough, she might understand what Max had done in response. She might want to pour water on Claire's room, too, or worse.

"I worked really hard on it," Max added.

"I'm sure you did," she said, bringing his head up and to her chest. He heard her heart, smelled her skin.

"I almost died. I was buried in the snow," he said, his words muffled in her shirt.

She held Max tighter now, and for a moment Max felt hopeful. He was no longer cold, and his face no longer burned. For a moment Max again forgot that he might be in trouble, and that trouble would come as soon as his mom walked into his sister's room.

"I'm sorry you had a bad day, Maxie," she said.

It sounded like she was actually sorry, but was she sorry enough to understand what Max had done in return? He avoided her eyes, though he could feel the heavy weight of their compassion.

"Where's Claire?" she asked.

"Who cares?" Max said.

"Who *cares*?" she laughed. "*I* do. And *you* should. She's supposed to be here. You can't be here alone after school. You both know that. Did she leave? I want to ask her about this igloo situation."

This conversation was becoming very satisfying. It hadn't occurred to Max until then that Claire was in trouble herself. She shouldn't have left! She was supposed to watch him but she had gone off in the ugly station wagon to chew tobacco. If Max was careful with this situation, he could divert all the attention to Claire's misdeeds.

But then came the sound of dripping.

"What's that?" his mom asked.

Max put on an unknowing face and shrugged.

His mom stood quickly. "Sounds like something's dripping. Did you take a bath?"

Max shook his head. He hadn't bathed; that was true.

She left the room. He could hear her in the bathroom, tightening the knobs on the tub. The drip persisted. "Where is that coming from?" she asked aloud.

Then she was in Claire's room.

She screamed.

Max never thought she would scream.

"What is this?" she shrieked.

This will be be hard, Max thought. *So hard.* He considered his options. He could make up a story about where the water came from. A hole in the roof? Maybe a window had been left open. He wished he'd thought of that sooner. Animals might have come in, tracking snow…

But he had never lied to his mom before and could not do it now. Instead, almost without thinking, he threw off the covers and got out of bed. He walked into Claire's room and heard the squish of the carpet under his feet. Standing in the doorway, her eyes wild, she saw the bucket and Max's snow clothes. She bent down to feel the floor and took in a quick breath.

"Did you do this?" she asked.

Max nodded and shrugged at the same time.

"Max, what were you *thinking*?"

He couldn't remember. His thoughts had scattered again, into a dozen tiny holes.

She ranted for a few minutes, using her most colorful language, before returning again to the question: "*What were you thinking?*"

"I don't know."

"You don't *know*?"

"It's hard to explain."

She was on her knees now. "This is not good, Max. All this water… It could soak into the beams. It could cause permanent damage to the house."

This news brought Max to the verge of tears. He wanted this to be temporary. He wanted it all over by dinner. Now the prospect that he'd ruined the house brought an endlessness to the day that crushed the light inside him.

She left the room. Max could hear the opening and slamming of cupboards as she cursed quietly to herself. She was gone a few long minutes. She returned with a pile of towels. "Come on. I'll help you clean it up."

They spread towels on the floor, trying to soak up the water. While they were on their knees, she noticed the water on the dolls, the pictures torn from the wall.

"Oh my god," she said. "The walls? The *walls*? What the hell is wrong with you?"

Max was wondering the same thing about himself.

She left the room and walked down the stairs. Max heard nothing for many minutes but he dared not move. He heard the car start, roar for a minute. Was she leaving? Then she turned off the engine. Finally he heard her walking up the stairs again and soon she was by his side again, on her knees, helping with the towels on the floor.

"What happened to you two?" she asked. "You used to be so close."

This made Max more sorry than before.

"I don't know," he mumbled.

She let out a sigh that filled the room. "I really need you to help keep this house together, Max," she said. "I need you to be a force of stability, not chaos."

Max nodded gravely. *Keep the house together. Force of stability.* On their hands and knees, Max and his mom continued to place towels on the carpet, trying to soak up the mess beneath them.

CHAPTER V

Max ate his dinner in his room, a plan of action that seemed the best for all concerned. He could hear Claire and his mom and Gary below, ticking and clicking their way through a quiet meal. He hadn't apologized yet and Claire hadn't either, and he was of the opinion that allowing the near-death of a brother was worse than soaking the room of a sister. After dinner he heard her leave, off to a babysitting job across the river.

When he was sure she was gone, Max stepped quietly into his mom's office in a corner of the back porch where she'd set up a desk and pair of bookshelves. The porch overlooked the back yard, black in the cold night, nothing out there but grey tree trunks, their bony fingers pinching brittle, shuddering leaves.

His mom was on the phone, typing on her computer, loudly, like someone pretending to type on a computer. Tap-tap, slip-tap, tap-tick-tap. Her long black hair fell forward, covering her cheeks; a strand was stuck to her lips. She seemed to notice Max but did not look directly at him.

He stepped down into the office, keeping close to the wall. He almost knocked a photo from where it hung, but steadied it. In it, a dozen of his mom's friends had gathered at a New Year's Eve party she'd had at the house. Max had been allowed to stay up until twelve, "running around like a friggin maniac" one of the friends had said, laughing, drinking his drink. Late in the night they had built a small fire in the backyard, roasting first a pig and later marsh-mallows, the guests drinking until they passed out all over the yard and living room and the bedrooms upstairs. The picture showed everyone sane and sober, but Max knew that things had changed later. Later he saw so many strange things: someone hiding in the bathroom, a fight between two of the men, adults on the floor everywhere, grabbing at each other and Max. Someone, at some point, went missing in the woods and wasn't found for hours. "Last time I do that," his mother said afterward, though it had been fun, everyone agreed, on balance.

With her phone conversation dragging on, it seemed like a good idea to begin crawling, so Max got down onto all fours and crawled along the edge of the wall until he made his way to the back window. He breathed heavily on the cold glass, making a rough oval of condensation. He drew an apple onto it, liking the crisp line his finger made.

On the phone, his mom's voice was thin and uncertain. "Do you know exactly what Holloway didn't like about the report?" she said, pulling the hair from her forehead.

Max's eyes fixed upon something under her desk: there was a red paper clip bent into the shape of a dragon. He did not want to attract attention, so he slithered, as slowly as he could, toward the paper clip and grabbed it. It was covered in a rubbery casing and felt good in his hands. With a similar length of rubber-covered wire, his father had once used a Swiss Army knife to cut the casing back and then twisted the metal into the shape of a swan. His father could do anything with a Swiss Army knife — or any knife, really. He would make things with his hands and then toss them to Max as if to say, It's just this thing. Take it if it means anything to you. Max had kept everything he'd ever made — swans, yo-yos, pull-toys, a kite made from vellum and sticks from the backyard.

"I just don't know where to begin," his mom said. "I feel like I have to start over and even then I don't know what he wants." Her voice quavered, and he wanted to do something to make her feel stronger. So often, when she seemed upset, when someone on the phone was making her cry, he didn't know what to do. But this night he thought he knew the solution.

He got up, and adopted the posture of a robot. He was very good at his robot imitation and had been told as much many times. He entered her peripheral vision, walking and sounding like a robot — a robot, he decided, who had a slight limp. She had laughed at this before, and he thought she might laugh today.

"I feel like that's what I did," his mom said into the phone. "Isn't that what I turned in?"

Finally she saw Max and forced a smile. He continued

walking, turning his head to smile at her, pretending that he was not noticing that he was about to walk into the wall. Thunk. He hit the wall. "Ohhh noo," he said, in a voice half robot, half Eeyore. "Ohhh noo," he groaned again, trying to walk through the wall, his robot arms rotating futilely.

She laughed, first silently, then out loud. She snorted. She had to cover the receiver to avoid being heard.

"That's okay," she said, recovering. "No problem. I guess I just have to get started. I'll have it in the morning. Thanks Candy. Sorry to call you at home. This'll be the last time. See you tomorrow."

She hung up the phone and looked over at Max.

"Come here," she said.

He stepped over to her, his forehead at the level of hers. Quickly she took Max in her arms and squeezed him. It was so sudden, though, and the hug was so intense — her arms almost vibrating — that Max let out a gasp.

"Oh Max. You make me happy," she said, kissing him roughly on the crown of his head. "You and Claire are the only things that keep me going."

Her hug became tighter, too tight to be meant for him only.

There was a long silence. Max wondered if he should say he was sorry, because he was sorry. But he could not find the word *Sorry*. He could only find words like *I want to live under my bed* and *Please take me back* and *Help*.

"Do you have a story for me?" she asked.

Max did not have a story ready.

"Yeah," he said, stretching out the word as long as he

could, while he thought of something. She liked to hear his stories, and would type them out on her computer as he narrated. Still searching for a tale, he lay down under the desk, the location where he usually did his narrating. He liked to be underneath, her feet resting on his stomach, where he could watch her face — to gauge her reaction to the story as it progressed — and to see her fingers on the keyboard. He needed to watch her type to make sure she was getting it all down.

He began:

"Once there were some buildings. They were these huge buildings and they could walk. So one day they got up and they left the city. Then there were some vampires. The vampires wanted to make the buildings into vampires so they flew in and attacked them. They bit them. One of the vampires bit the tallest building but his fangs broke off. Then the rest of his teeth fell out. And he cried because he would never get new teeth again. And the other vampires said *Why are you crying, aren't those just your baby teeth?* And the vampire said *No, those are my grown-up teeth.* And the vampires knew he couldn't be a vampire anymore, so they left him. And he couldn't be friends with the buildings because the vampires had killed them all."

"Is that the end?" his mom asked.

"Yeah," Max said.

His mom finished typing and smiled sadly down at Max.

"The end," he said.

She continued to rub his stomach with her foot. It felt good and terrible and he was so tired, so very tired, so incredibly tired all over.

CHAPTER VI

A quiet, cream-colored morning. Max stayed in bed until Claire was gone, then slipped into her room. Her bedspread had, for now, been replaced by a sleeping bag. Her wall, where he had soaked her photo collages, was stripped clean. In his bare feet, he could feel the cold water still in the carpet. He knelt and rested his head on the floor. He could hear no creaking in the beams, no signs of permanent damage. But there were dangers, he was sure, that could not be seen or heard, structural weaknesses that might suddenly give way.

Downstairs, Max sat alone on the couch, eating his breakfast — cereal, grapefruit juice, and two bananas. He was reading the sports section of the newspaper, a habit his father had encouraged; when Max was not yet two he began eating his breakfast next to his dad in the morning, the two of them nestled in a corner of the couch, reading the comics and then the sports and sometimes the real estate section.

"Hey Max," Gary said from the kitchen. "You know where your mom keeps the coffee?"

"In the cabinet under the sink," Max said.

He heard Gary open that cabinet and close it.

"You sure?"

This was the one pleasure Max took from having Gary in the house. Gary couldn't remember where anything was in the kitchen, and seemed to be the most gullible adult Max had ever met. This made it far too easy for Max to hide something different every day, some different essential element of Gary's breakfast, and then pretend to help him find it. One day it was the coffee; another day the filters; another day the lemonade Gary liked to drink; another day the little scooper Gary needed to determine the correct dosage of lemonade crystals in his glass. One day Max replaced Gary's new English muffins with the molding ones his mother had just thrown out. Another day Max put the butter in the freezer, and heard, from the couch, Gary ruining his muffin while forcing the ice-hard butter into the muffin's nooks and crannies.

"Maybe the one by the hall?" Max said.

Gary opened the cabinet by the hallway, spent some time looking inside, and finally Max heard it close.

"Wait. I think maybe the fridge," Max said. "Mom read something about refrigerating it, how you're supposed to."

"Thanks bud," Gary said. And so the fridge opened and closed. A minute later: "Darn," he said. "I thought we had it that time."

"Aw, shoot," Max said.

And the great thing was that whenever Max played the

game — only a few times a week, so as to avoid arousing suspicion — Gary seemed to think that the two of them were in it together, that Max was doing everything in his power to help. In Gary's mind, they'd bonded.

"Oh well," Gary said, entering the foyer. "Guess I'll have to spring for the real thing at Monaco's, eh?"

Max nodded, not having any idea what that meant, and returned to his newspaper. A few seconds later he looked up to find Gary sitting on the bench near the front door. Max had never thought to sit on this bench, which was used for papers, mail, and other things on their way into drawers or out the door. At the moment it was also home to a delicate bird of clay that Max had made in art class, blue and with a dozen toothpicks extending from its torso; the art teacher, Mr. Hjortness, had called it the Blowfish Bluebird, and Max liked that name a lot. Now Gary gently but quickly swept the bird aside to make way for his buttocks. Next he reached down, fumbling for something under the bench. There were many shoes under the bench, all of them his or his mom's or Claire's. Now Gary's shoes dwelled there, too, and it didn't seem right.

"Hey Max," he said, while not looking at Max. He was tying his small shoes — they looked like eels, narrow and made of cheap black pleather — and saying, "Max... Max... What rhymes with Max?"

Max didn't care what rhymed with Max. He wanted Gary to first stop talking, then to leave the house.

Gary, now done with his shoes, looked up. "Hey Max. You know where your mom keeps any tools?"

Max had never seen tools in the house. At least not since his father had left.

"Have you tried the kitchen?" Max said, suppressing a laugh. He heard Gary start toward the kitchen and then stop.

"The kitchen? What would a hammer be doing in the kitchen?" Gary asked. He really had no sense of humor at all, thank god.

Now he was in front of Max again. He was looking out the window, at his car, a crumbling white sedan. "Not that I'm 'handy' or anything," he said, making a crank-turning gesture intended to mean "handy." "I can't get my trunk open. I need a big hammer or something. Sometimes you just need a hammer to get down to real business, am I right or am I right?"

Max couldn't think of a good answer to that round of nonsense, so he went back to his sports section.

"Oh well," Gary said, as he shoved his pale, freckled arms through the sleeves of his jacket. "Another day, huh?"

Max shrugged again without looking up.

Gary took a few steps toward him; he was suddenly far too close. "Listen. I'm, like, trying to make your mom happy."

Max's face went hot. Every so often Gary decided to make such a pronouncement, a statement meant to define exactly why he was sleeping in their home three or so nights a week. And always Max wanted these moments over as soon as possible. He felt Gary close, standing to his right, trying to catch Max's eye. Max stared so intensely at his cereal that he felt sure he could see the microscopic chemical compounds that formed each flake.

"Whatever," Gary finally said. He walked over to the stairs. "See ya Connie," he yelled.

"What?" his mother yelled down the stairs.

Gary mumbled something to himself and, returning to the foyer, began looking for something in his pockets. He didn't find it, so he eyed the change bowl on the bench. It was a silver bowl, evidence of some anniversary, and it was always full of coins, safety pins, barrettes, pens and pencils. And now it was filled with Gary's soft pink hand. Max watched as Gary's fingers made their way through the bright coins, slithering in every direction. Like the tentacles of a squid bringing food into its gaping maw, the fingers gathered ten or so quarters into the sweaty center of his Gary's fist. He deposited the bounty into his front pants pocket and left.

Seconds later, Max's mom appeared in the foyer, head tilted, installing an earring.

"Someone yelled upstairs," she said. "Was that you?"

Max shook his head. Together they looked outside. Gary was folding himself into his old white car, licked everywhere by rust. With a cough of blue smoke, it shook to life and Gary was gone.

CHAPTER VII

"You ready?" his mom asked.

Max didn't want to be driven to school, but he had no choice. His school had done away with bus service. There were only a handful of kids whose parents had allowed them to ride it in the first place, and so the previous year they'd gotten rid of it entirely. No one complained, no one missed it.

Riding his bike to school was no longer an option. After he'd been biking to school for a month, one of the parents, Mr. Neimenov, had complained. First to Max's mom, then Max's dad, and finally to the principal. He thought that Max's unchaperoned riding was attracting potential child-abductors and child-assaulters. "Just as a liquor store attracts drunks," he'd written in a note to Max's mom, "so does an 8-year-old riding alone attract all kinds of unsavory types…"

When Max's parents hadn't responded, Mr. Neimenov

brought the matter up with the school, and they quickly gave in. It wasn't even a battle. There wasn't a bike rack on the grounds in the first place. Max had been the only one who'd been riding to school.

The good thing about Thursdays was that on Thursdays there was gym. Thursdays were the only day, in fact, when gym occurred. And given budget cutbacks and new priorities and bi-weekly all-school testing sessions, there were only twelve gym days a year. So Max knew to savor each one. He ran out to the blacktop — the school had paved over the grass to save money to buy more Scantron forms — and lined up.

"Okay folks," Mr. Ichythis said to the class, "as you know, we have only one day for each sport, so today's our day to cover soccer. We use this ball for soccer," he said, holding up a volleyball, "and the object is to kick it into that net." He pointed to one of the goals, then seemed suddenly to notice something. "Or that one," he said, nodding toward the opposite goal. "Either one, I guess."

With that, he blew his whistle and threw the ball in the air. The kids immediately scattered. Half ran toward the ball, the other half for the sidelines.

There were only a handful of kids emotionally prepared, Max had learned, for team sports. And even some of the seemingly athletic kids were prone to bursts of crying. Wherever there was a ball and a net — soccer, basketball, tennis — crying followed. Even in his weekend soccer league, in every practice and every game, there were kids weeping. They cried when they were touched, they cried when they missed the ball, they cried when the other team scored. They cried when faced with any possible doubt or disappointment. They cried as a default, they cried when they didn't know what else to do.

But Max knew what to do. He was on the soccer field to kick, chase, survey, run, slide-tackle, and score at will. When he was playing, he felt a sense of self-possession and order that was unparalleled anywhere else in his life. He knew where the ball was going; he knew where the other players were and where they were likely to go; at any given moment he knew exactly what had to be done.

He also had a sense of what needed to be stopped, and when. At that very moment, Dan Cooper was heading down the sidelines, dribbling the ball toward the goal. It would be up to Max to stop this business, so he made himself a torpedo and plugged in Dan's coordinates. Max was quickly upon him, and when he was within striking distance, and Dan was about to score on the open net — the goalie was hiding behind the goalpost — Max unleashed unto Dan Cooper a slide-tackle of great ferocity and terrible accuracy.

Max was heading the opposite direction, careening upfield with the ball and praying that Dan wouldn't cry, when the whistle stopped him.

"Foul," Mr. Ichythis said.

The slide-tackle had been legal but the kids on the sidelines were giving Max disapproving looks. "Savage," one girl hissed. Dan was indeed crying, silently, deeply, as if lamenting all the sadness and injustice in the world.

"What kind of foul?" Max asked.

"The penalty kind," Mr. Ichythis said.

"For what?" Max asked.

"For making Dan fall," Mr. Ichythis said. "Just go to the penalty box and give me a break, okay?"

There was no such thing as a penalty box in this sport, but Max didn't feel like explaining it all to him. To a chorus of judgmental frowns from the non-participating girls and boys, Max walked off the field and into the school. It was almost lunch anyway.

In science class, Mr. Wisner had just discussed the sad plight of Pluto, the smallest and most remote planet, which had long languished on the periphery of the universe, and now was a planet no more. It was now just some rock in space.

Max was staring up at the model universe dangling from the ceiling when something Mr. Wisner was saying caught his attention.

"Of course," he was saying, "the sun is the center of our solar system. It's why all of the planets are here. It creates day and night and the warmth of its sunlight is what makes our planet inhabitable. Of course, the sun won't always be here to warm us. Like all things, the sun will die. When it does, it'll first expand, and will envelop all the planets around it, including the Earth, which it will consume rapidly…"

Max didn't like the sound of any of this. He looked around. None of the other students seemed to be listening closely.

Mr. Wisner continued: "The sun, after all, is just fuel,

burning ferociously, and when our particular star — a painfully average one, I should say — runs out of fuel, our solar system will go dark, permanently…"

Max had a sick feeling in his stomach. There was something about the words *go dark permanently* that didn't sit well with him. This was the very worst lesson Max had ever heard in school, and there were fifteen minutes left on the clock. Mr. Wisner turned and pulled down a map of the world.

"But before that, the human race will likely fall to one of any number of calamities — self-inflicted or not: war, radical climate change, meteors, spectacular floods and earthquakes, superviruses…"

Now he turned back to the students, with a look on his face that was almost cheerful.

"Wow, I sound like a downer, don't I! Look on the bright side — you and everyone you know will be long gone by then! When the sun is extinguished and the world is swallowed like a grape by the collapsing fabric of space, we'll be long forgotten in the endless continuum of time. The human race is, after all, just a sigh in the long sonorous sleep of this world and all worlds to come. Okay, that's the end for today. Have a great weekend."

CHAPTER VIII

Max was often the last one picked up, but it didn't matter so much. He was bored most of the time he was at A Spoonful of Lovin' Afterschool Centre, so it was no big deal to be bored while waiting for his mom to pick him up. He sat on the steps of the porch, listening for his mom's car to gag and shimmy around the corner.

He'd been going to this center for a year. The previous one he went to had gotten too uptight about money, his mom said, so one day he'd switched to this one, which, she said, had a more *humane* payment plan.

The man in charge of A Spoonful of Lovin' was short and slight and named Perry. He was trying to grow a beard, but he looked like a mangy dog; none of the growth areas on his face connected.

When Max's mom pulled in, Perry waved and walked to his own car. "Good night, Max."

Max didn't run to his mom's car and didn't walk slowly, either. In this way the walk seemed to last weeks.

Max got into the car and closed the door. He sat in the front seat because he got the front once a week.

"Hey Maxie," his mom said, rubbing his knee.

"Hey," he said.

"Hi Mr. Perry," she said, waving. "That's gonna cost me twenty dollars," she said to Max as she pulled away. Every minute late cost a dollar. That was the rule.

Claire was in the back, her feet propped up on the back of Max's seat. She didn't even look Max's way, so he said nothing to her. It was obvious that neither of them would back down and apologize, and Max guessed it would be like a hundred other fights they'd had: it would be placed, precariously, in the crowded closet of all they'd done to each other, safe behind the door until someone turned the knob again.

Now that they were moving again, she picked up a conversation begun before Max's arrival.

"You're really not coming?" Claire said, seeming astonished. They were talking about some kind of talent show that she was going to be in.

"I can't, Claire," Max's mom said, "I can't take the afternoon off. Not right now. You know that. Put your seatbelt on."

Claire ignored this directive. "Why don't you just quit? Tell Holloway to F off?"

They were talking about Mom's boss. They were often talking about Mom's boss. Claire knew everything about Mom's job and advised her on how to handle it.

"I thought we decided I'd stick this out for at least a year and then— "

"But he's not taking you seriously," Claire interrupted. "You said he's supposed to give you a raise if you finished the course. At the review he said— "

"I know, but don't you think— "

"I talked to Dad and he said you should— "

"Don't!" Mom barked. "*Don't...*" she repeated, taking a deep breath and clenching her fists. "*Don't* talk to your father about my job. He has too many opinions about me. I know you and he think this house is a failure, Claire, but he's one voice I don't need right now..."

Max was so tired of this kind of argument that he didn't know what to say or think. He had tried to stop these discussions before but all that had happened was that the two of them turned on him at once, and he didn't want that. Better to wait it out. Something grabbed his mother's attention.

"Huh," she said, looking out the window. "See that? You know what that is, Max? Hold your breath." The traffic was stopped on three sides of the intersection as a line of black cars drove by. Max held his breath.

After the cars were gone, it occurred to Max to tell his mother about what he'd learned in Mr. Wisner's class.

"We did planets today."

His mom said nothing. Claire said nothing. It was as if Max hadn't actually spoken. But he was sure he had spoken.

"Did you hear?" Max said.

His mom was squinting into the distance, as if still

arguing, in her mind, with Claire, or her boss, or with Max's father. She did this every day, usually while driving.

"Mr. Wisner said the sun's gonna die," Max said. "After you and me and everyone's gone." He looked to his mother for some response, but the profundity of what he said seemed to have no effect at all. "Did you know that?" he asked.

Still no response. He turned around to Claire, but her eyes were closed. Tinny music escaped from her white headphones.

Max turned back to his mom. "Can we stop it?"

Now his mom turned to him, finally focusing all her attention.

"You know, Max," she said, "I really hope you treat women decently. I hope you never have a relationship with a woman you don't respect."

This didn't seem to have anything to do with planets or the sun, but Max thought about it for a second and answered, more quietly than he intended, "Okay."

The black cars now gone, she pulled into the intersection.

"Really," she said. "I mean it."

"I won't," Max said. "Or I will." He couldn't remember which way he was supposed to answer.

They drove in silence for a while. Max began deciphering the message his mom had given him. She did this periodically, tossing similar sorts of advice to him. He had starting writing it down, hoping it would make sense at some future date.

"Just try and be a decent person," she added, finishing

the matter. He nodded and looked out the window, spotting the city far beyond, the city where his father lived, looking like a tiny pile of grey rocks in the sea.

CHAPTER IX

Max decided to go for a quick bike ride before dinner. He was going to tell his mom he was leaving, but then didn't, oh well. She was busy with Gary anyway. He was lounging on the couch, drinking red wine and watching one of their musicals. Every night was some musical.

Max burst out into the cold night and sped down the driveway. He had to think and he could only think while biking or building things, and he wanted to be biking, to think with the blood loudly filling his head.

He rode one-handed, then no-handed, then with his head slung back, squinting at the emerging stars. He whistled quietly to himself, then louder, then hummed, then sang out loud. It was a quiet night and he wanted to slash it open with his own voice.

"Aw, shut up, you," a voice said.

Max recognized the voice. It was Mr. Beckmann. Max had just passed him and his dog, Achilles.

Max circled his bike around.

"*You* shut up, old bones," Max said.

Mr. Beckmann laughed out loud. He was an older man, maybe eighty or a hundred, who lived down the road and was often seen walking, slowly and steadily, for hours at a time, through the streets and paths and forests, always with Achilles, a dog easily as big as Max and with an aristocratic bearing. The animal was so perfectly bred and well cared for it looked like a dictionary etching of a German shepard. Achilles knew Max well and was already laying on his side, urging Max to scratch his stomach.

Max dropped his bike and did so.

"So Maximilian," Mr. Beckmann said. "How the hell are you?"

"Okay I guess," Max answered. "I got in trouble again."

"Oh yeah? What'd you do this time?"

Mr. Beckmann's eyes were dangerously alive, punctuated by brows so thick and mischievously arched that he seemed at all times to be plotting a great and dastardly plan.

Max told him about soaking Claire's room with the water.

"What'd you use?" Mr. Beckmann asked. "A bucket?"

Max nodded.

"Yeah, I would have used a bucket, too."

This is why Max loved Mr. Beckmann: he was an equal. He seemed to have navigated his way through seven or so decades of adulthood without forgetting one moment of his childhood — what he loved and hated, feared and coveted.

Max and Mr. Beckmann stood for a long moment,

breathing their loud grey breaths into the still night.

Max had visited Mr. Beckmann's house a few times, and had walked carefully through, fascinated by his collection of strange old toys and posters. Mr. Beckmann had a thing for King Kong, and had collected various souvenirs and models from the movie's first incarnation. There were also delicate tin toys, Mickey Mouse and Little Nemo, in glass displays. There were huge books full of paintings and all throughout the house, most of the time, was music, something classical, stringy, and bright.

The last time Max had been there, Mr. Beckmann had answered the phone and Max had overheard a colorful argument between the old man and one of the street's new neighbors. This new neighbor apparently was objecting to the run-down barn in Mr. Beckmann's backyard. It was a barn Max often played in, and where he had stored his wristrocket and M-80s. The man on the phone saw it as an eyesore and was apparently offering to remove it for Mr. Beckmann. Mr. Beckmann did not like the idea so much. "If I hear from you again," he yelled at the phone, "I'll hire a crane, pick that barn up, come over to your house, and drop that barn on your head."

Max laughed, knowing that would be the end of that particular neighbor's complaints. Then he and Mr. Beckmann had eaten ice cream sandwiches.

"So you're in trouble. So what?" Mr. Beckmann said, his breath visible, cloaking him. "Boys are supposed to get in trouble. Look at you. You're built for trouble."

Max smiled. "Yeah, but Gary said— "

"What?" Mr. Beckmann interrupted. "Who the hell's Gary?"

Max explained who Gary was, or who he thought Gary was. Mr. Beckmann shook his head dismissively.

"Well I don't like him already. What kind of name is Gary, anyway? Sounds like a carny. Is he a carny?"

Max laughed.

"Gary Schmary," Mr. Beckmann said. "You want me to sic Achilles on him? He'd swallow Gary Schmary in one bite."

Max thought this was a pretty good idea, but shook his head. "No, that's okay."

They stood in the night. Far off, a dog or wolf howled. Mr. Beckmann was looking up at the broad silver stripe across the dome of the sky.

Mr. Beckmann started down toward his house. "Well, I'll be seeing you, Maximilian."

"See you, Mr. Beckmann," Max said.

Mr. Beckmann stopped, remembering something. "Remember, Achilles is always ready to eat some Gary."

Max laughed and rode home to eat dinner.

CHAPTER X

Max knew that a bunk bed was the perfect structure to use when building an indoor fort. First of all, bunk beds have a roof. And a roof was essential if you're going to have an observation tower. And you need an observation tower if you're going to spot invading armies before they breach your walls and overtake your kingdom. Anyone without bunks would have a much harder time maintaining a security perimeter, and if you can't do that, you don't stand a chance against anyone.

Max had just done a quick survey of the area surrounding his bunk-kingdom and now was down below on the lower bunk, where he could be unseen and unknown. For a while he thought about the sun and whether it would die. He thought about whether he would die someday, too. It was a very strange time in Max's life. His sister had tried, by proxy, to kill him, and his mother didn't seem to care about that or the end of the universe. On this evening, the person in the house he seemed to like the most was Gary, and even thinking that sent a shudder through him. He wondered if Mr. Beckmann would allow him to live at his house, and if not, in the barn that he'd threatened his neighbors about.

Max, tired of thinking, decided to think on paper, and so retrieved his journal from under the bed. His father had given him the journal shortly after he left, and had, in white-out, written the words WANT JOURNAL on the cover. *In this book*, his father had written as inscription and directive, *write what you want. Every day, or as often as you can, write what you want. That way, whenever you're confused or rudderless, you can look to this book, and be reminded where you want to go and what you're looking for.* His father had written, by hand, three beginnings on every page. Every page started with:

I WANT

I WANT

I WANT

And so Max had periodically written his wants, and he'd written many other things, too. But tonight he wanted to write some more wants, so he found a pen and began.

I WANT *Gary to fall into some kind of bottomless hole.*

I WANT *Claire to get her foot caught in a beartrap.*

I WANT *Claire's friends to die by flesh-eating tapeworms.*

Then he stopped. His father had reminded him that the journal was for positive wants, not negative wants. When you wanted something *negative*, it didn't count, he said. A want should be positive, his father had said. A want should improve your life while improving the world, even if just a little bit.

So Max began again:

I WANT *to get out of here.*

I WANT *to go to the moon or some other planet.*

I WANT *to find some unicorn DNA and then grow a bunch of them and teach them to stick their horns through Claire's friends.*

Oh well. He could erase it later. For now just writing it and thinking it felt good. But now he was sick of writing. He wanted to make something. But he didn't want to set up some whole thing with glue and wood. He didn't want to have to use tools at all. What did he want to do? This was the central question of this day and most days.

Max wondered how he might actually build a ship. He had designed many dozens of ships on paper over the past year, and now he wondered if it was time for him to build a real one and sail away. His father had taken him sailing five times the previous summer, and had taught him the basics of piloting a small boat. "You're a natural!" his father had said, even though Max was afraid of the open water, of rogue waves and orcas.

Then Max caught sight of his wolf suit, hanging on the back of the closet door. He hadn't worn it in weeks. He'd gotten it for Christmas three years before, the last one with both his parents, and he'd immediately put it on, and kept it on for the rest of school break. It had been too big then, but his mom had pinned it and taped it to make it work until he grew into it.

Now he and it were the perfect size and he wore it

when he knew he would be alone in the house, and when he could wrestle the dog or jump and growl without anyone watching. And though the house was full, as Max stared at the wolf suit it seemed to be calling to him. *It's time*, it was saying to Max. He wasn't sure this was actually the right time to put it on, but then again he'd never disobeyed the suit before. Should he really wear it tonight? He usually felt better when he put on the wolf suit. He felt faster, sleeker, more powerful.

On the other hand, he could stay in bed. He could stay in the fort, the red blanket casting a red light on everything inside. He had stayed inside one whole weekend a few months ago. He couldn't remember why he'd done this. Or maybe he could remember. Maybe it had to do with Claire and Meika and how they laughed when he had gone into the bathroom with his hand down his pants. They were sitting on Claire's bed, and it was the morning, and in the morning he had been in the habit of having his hand down his pajama pants. So he had walked into the bathroom to pee and they had laughed for what seemed like hours. And he hadn't put his hand down his pants since then.

Anyway, he had hid in his bedroom fort for two days after that. Mom had brought his meals to him there and he had played Stratego against himself, and cards against himself, and had pitted his animals and soldiers against each other, and had read two books about medieval wars.

Now he wondered if he wanted to just spend another weekend in his fort. It seemed a good enough idea. He had some thinking to do, about this news about the sun expiring and the resulting void inhaling the earth, and he wanted to steer clear of Claire, who might yet want retribution, and he was angry at his mom, who seemed to forget for hours at a time that he existed. And any time he spent in his room ensured that he didn't have to talk to Gary.

So he had a choice. Would he stay behind the curtain and think about things, marinate in his own confusion, or would he put on his white fur suit and howl and scratch and make it known who was boss of this house and all of the world known and unknown?

CHAPTER XI

"Arooooooo!"

The howling was a good start. Animals howl, he had been told, to declare their existence. Max, standing in his white wolf suit, stood at the top of the stairs and, using a rolled-up piece of construction paper as a megaphone, howled again, as loud as he could.

"ARRROOOOOOOOOOOOOOO!"

When he was done, there was a long silence.

"Uh oh," Gary finally said.

Ha! Max thought. *Let Gary worry. Let everyone worry.*

Max pounded down the stairs, triumphant. "Who wants to get eaten?" he asked the house and the world.

"Not me," Claire said.

Aha! Max decided. *That only puts her higher on the menu!*

He strode into the TV room, where Claire was pretending to do her homework. He lifted his claws up, growled and sniffed at the air. He wanted to make sure that

Claire and everyone knew this terrible fact: There was a bloodthirsty, brilliant, borderline-insane wolf in their midst.

Claire didn't look up.

At least she'd spoken to him. It was a window to reconciliation, so Max had an idea. He removed a wooden dowel from a nearby curtain. It was about three feet long and bore magic marker lines across its width. Claire, seeing Max approach with the dowel, rolled her eyes.

"You want to play Wolf and Master?" Max asked.

Claire had already gone back to her book, strenuously ignoring him. She didn't even need to say No. She could say No a thousand ways without ever uttering the word.

"Why not?" Max said to the back of her head.

"Maybe because your wolf suit smells like butt?"

Max quickly sniffed himself. She was correct. But he *was* a wolf. What else would a wolf smell like?

"You want me to kill something for you?" he asked.

Claire thought a moment, tapping her pencil against her lower teeth. Finally she looked at Max, her eyes bright. "Yeah," she said, "go kill the little man in the living room."

This idea had a certain appeal. Max smiled at Claire's description of Gary as a "little man."

"Yeah," Max said, getting excited. "We'll cut his brains out and make him eat 'em! He'll have to think from his stomach!"

Claire gave Max a look she might give a three-headed cat. "Yeah, you go do that," she said.

Max walked around the corner and found Gary lying on the couch in his work clothes, his frog-eyes closed, his chin entirely receded into his neck. Max gritted his teeth and let out a low, simmering growl.

Gary opened his eyes and rubbed them.

"Uhh, hey Max. I'm baggin' a few after-work Zs. How goes it?"

Max looked at the floor. This was one of Gary's typical questions: *Another day, huh? How goes it? No play for the playa, right?* None of his questions had answers. Gary never seemed to say anything that meant anything at all.

"Cool suit," Gary said. "Maybe I'll get me one of those. What are you, like a rabbit or something?"

Max was about to leap upon Gary, to show him just what kind of animal he was — a wolf capable of tearing flesh from bone with a shake of his jaws — when Max's mom came into the room. She was carrying two glasses of blood-colored wine, and she handed one to Gary. Gary sat up, smiled his powerless smile, and clinked his glass against hers. It was a disgusting display, and became more so when Gary raised his glass to Max.

"Cheers, little rabbit-dude," he said.

His mom smiled at Max and then at Gary, thinking it was a wonderfully clever thing that Gary had just said.

"Cheers, Maxie," she said, then growled playfully at him.

She picked up a dirty plate and hurried back toward the kitchen. "Claire!" she yelled. "I asked you to get your stuff off the table. It's almost dinner."

Max entered the kitchen with his arms crossed, marching purposefully, like a general inspecting his troops. He sniffed loudly, assessing the kitchen's smells and waiting to be noticed.

His mother said nothing, so he brought a chair near the stove and stood on it. Now they were eye to eye.

"What is that? Is that food?" he asked, pointing down to something beige bubbling in a pan.

He got no answer.

"Mom, what is that?" he asked, now grabbing her arm.

"Pâté," she said finally.

Max rolled his eyes and moved on. Pâté was a regrettable name for an unfortunate food. It seemed to Max a good idea to get up from the chair and to leap onto the counter. Which he presently did.

Standing on the counter, he towered over everything and everyone. He was eleven feet tall.

"Oh god," Max's mom said.

Max squatted down to inspect a package of frozen corn. "Frozen corn? What's wrong with *real* corn?" he demanded. He dropped the package loudly on the counter, where it made a wonderful clatter.

"Frozen corn *is* real," Max's mom said, barely taking notice. "Now get off the counter. And go tell your sister to get her stuff off the dining room table."

Max didn't move. "CLAIRE GET YOUR STUFF OFF THE DINING ROOM TABLE!" he yelled, more or less into his mom's face.

"Don't yell in my face!" she hissed. "And get off the counter."

Instead of getting off the counter, Max howled. The acoustics where he was, so close to the ceiling, were not great.

His mom stared at him like he was crazy. Which he was, because wolves are part crazy. "You know what," she said, "you're too old to be on the counter, and you're too old to be wearing that costume."

Max crossed his arms and stared down at her. "You're too old to be so short! And your makeup's smeared!"

"Get DOWN from there!" she demanded.

The sting of what she had said about him being too old to wear his wolf suit was just hitting him. He felt his anger focusing. There was a weakness in her voice and he decided to seize on it.

"Woman, feed me!" he yelled. He didn't know where he'd come up with that phrase, but he liked it immediately.

"Get off the counter, Max!"

Max just stared at her. She was so small!

"I'll eat you up!" he growled, raising his arms.

"MAX! GET DOWN!" she yelled. She could be very loud when she wanted to be. For a second he thought he should get off the counter, take off his suit, and eat his dinner quietly, because the truth was he was very hungry. But then he thought better of it, and howled again.

"Arooooooooo!"

At that, Max's mom lunged for him, but Max, side-stepping, was able to elude her grasp. He leaped over the sink and then back down onto the chair. She lunged again and missed. Max cackled. He really was fast! She grabbed at him again, but he was already gone. He jumped down, landed on the floor, and executed a perfect shoulder-roll. Then he got up and fled from the kitchen altogether, laughing hysterically.

When he turned around, though, he found that his mom was still chasing him. That was new. She rarely chased him this far. When they raced through the living room, Gary took notice of the escalating volume and urgency. He put down his glass of wine and got ready to intervene.

Then, in the front hall, a surprising and awful thing happened: Max's mom caught him.

"Max!" she gasped.

She had his arm firmly in her hand. She had long fingers, deceptively strong, and they dug into Max's bicep. In her hand all his muscle and sinew turned to soup and he didn't like it.

"What's wrong with you?" she screamed. "You see what you're doing to me?" Her voice was shrill, corkscrewed.

"No, *you're* doing things!" he countered, sounding meeker than he'd intended. To offset this sign of weakness he thrashed around in her grip. He kicked and squirmed and in the process, he knocked everything off the bench — the change, the mail, and his delicate blue bird, the one he'd made in art class. It broke and like quail the pieces darted to every corner of the foyer.

This gave them both pause.

They stared at the broken bird.

"See that? You're out of control!" she said. "There's no way you're eating dinner with us. Animal."

Now, because he was angry at breaking his bird, and angry at having Gary in the house, and angry at having to eat pâté and frozen corn and angry about having a witch for a sister, he growled and squirmed and — the idea flooded him so quickly he couldn't resist — leaned down and bit his mom's arm as hard as he could.

She screamed and dropped him to the floor. She stepped back, still holding her arm. She wailed like a beast, her eyes alive with fear and fury.

Max had never bitten her before. He was scared. His mom was scared. They saw each other anew.

Max turned to see Gary entering the foyer. He was clearly unsure what he was supposed to do.

"Connie, are you okay?" he asked.

"He bit me!" she hissed.

Gary's eyes bulged. He had no idea what to do or say. The sheer number of things happening was overwhelming him. He opened his mouth and did the best he could: "You can't let him treat you that way!" he said.

Max's mom gave him a bewildered look.

"What are you talking about? This is about *me*? What do you want me to do?"

"Something! Something needs to be done!" Gary said, taking a few quick strides toward Max.

"*He's* not allowed to talk here!" Max yelled, pointing to the frog-eyed man.

Claire stormed into the hall at that second, and seeing Claire and Gary and his mom, everyone looking at him like *he* was the problem — it sent Max tumbling over the edge. He screamed as loud as he could — a sound between a howl and a battle cry.

"Why are you doing this to me?" his mom wailed. "This house is chaos with you in it!"

That was it. Max did not have to stand for this, any of this, all of this. He threw open the door and leapt down the porch and into the night.

CHAPTER XII

The air! The moon!

Both opened to him immediately. He felt pulled as if by an outgoing tide. The air and moon together sang a furious and wonderful song: *Come with us, wolf-boy! Let us drink the blood of the earth and gargle it with great aplomb!* Max tore down the street, feeling free, knowing he was part of the wind. *Come, Max! Come to the water and see!* No one could tell that he was crying — he was running too fast. He left the yard and took to the street.

"Max!"

Stupid Gary was following him, trying to run, huffing mightily. Max ran faster, almost flying, his hands grabbing at the air as he passed all the homes being rebuilt from scratch, the mess of them all. When he looked over his shoulder, he saw that Gary was losing ground. A moment later, the freckled little man had pulled up lame — he was doubled over, holding his leg. Max kept running, and though his face was wet with tears, he grinned maniacally. He had won. He ran to the cul-de-sac, where the road ended and the trees began.

Max was free of home and mother and Gary and Claire, he had outwitted and outrun them all, but he was not ready to rest. He ran to his lean-to, and sat inside for a few seconds, but was too alive to sit still. He got up and howled. Something about the wind and the configuration of the trees and outcroppings gave his voice more volume; his howl twisted and multiplied in the sky in the most satisfying way. He howled more.

He grabbed the biggest stick he could find and commenced hitting everything he could with it. He swung it around, he stabbed trees and rocks, he whacked branches and relieved them of their snowy burden.

This, he thought, was the only way he wanted to live. He would live from now on here in the woods. All he needed to do, sometime soon, would be to sneak back into the house and get more of his things — his knives, some matches, some blankets and glue and rope. Then he would build a forest home, high in the trees, and become one with the woods and the animals, learn their languages and with them plot an overthrow of his home, beginning with the decapitation and devouring of Gary.

As he planned his new life, he heard a sound. It wasn't the wind and it wasn't the trees. It was a scraping, yearning sound. He paused, his nose and ears pricking up. Again he heard it. It was like bone against bone, though there was a rhythm to it. He followed it toward the water, a hundred yards away. He jogged down the ravine and met the stream that led to the shore. He jumped from rock to rock until he saw the bay's black glass, cut through the middle by the reflection of the moon.

At the water's edge, amid the reeds and the softly lapping waves, he saw the source of the noise: a wooden sailboat of average size and painted white. It was tied to a tree and was rubbing against a half-submerged rock.

Max looked around to see if anyone was close. It seemed strange that a boat like this, a sturdy, viable boat, would be unoccupied. He had been coming to this bay for years and had never seen a boat like this, alone and without an owner. There was no sign of anyone near. The boat was his if he wanted it.

CHAPTER XIII

He stepped in. There was just a bit of water on the floor, and when he checked the rudder and sail and boom, everything seemed to be in working order.

If he wanted to, he could untie the boat and sail out into the bay. It would be better than just living out his days in the forest. He could sail away, as far as he liked. He might make it somewhere new, somewhere better, and if he didn't — if he drowned in the bay or the ocean beyond — then so be it. His horrible family would have to live forever with the guilt. Either option seemed good.

He reached back toward shore, untied the boat from the tree, and pushed off.

He righted the boat and aimed it toward the center of the bay. He unfurled the sail and steadied the boom. The wind was strong; in no time he was chopping through the bay's small waves, heading due north.

He had sailed at night only once before, with his father, and even that had been unplanned. They'd gotten stuck out in the bay without wind, and hadn't brought a paddle. They'd passed the time naming every candy they could remember and playing hangman with a grease marker on the boat's floor. It occurred to Max at that moment that he didn't have any of the safety items his father insisted on — a life preserver, a paddle, a flare gun, a bailing vessel. The boat was empty but for Max.

And he was getting cold. Max was wearing only his wolf suit, and by the time he reached the middle of the bay and the wind began to bite, he realized that it was December, and no more than forty degrees, and it was getting colder the farther out into the lake he ventured. When he'd been running and howling, he hadn't felt the rip of the winter wind, but now it cut through his fur — and his T-shirt and underwear, for that's all he was wearing underneath — unimpeded.

He wouldn't be able to sail this way for long. He certainly wouldn't make it through the night; his teeth were already chattering. So he decided to sail not into the ocean but toward the city, to head to his father's place downtown. This immediately seemed a better idea all around. He would sail downtown, dock with all the yachts, walk through the city until he found his father's apartment, and ring the bell.

Wow, he'd be surprised! He knew his father would be proud of him when he arrived. He'd be astounded and impressed and they would live together from then on. All he needed to do was sail north for a few hours and keep his eye on the lights in the distance. He could make out the dim glow of the city on the horizon, and he felt strong again, knowing he would soon be there.

CHAPTER XIV

But the city seemed to be getting farther away, not closer. For hours Max held the rudder steady, and the sail had a constant belly full of wind, but as the hours passed, the city grew smaller. According to the compass, Max was sailing directly for it, due north-northwest, and yet the city lights were growing smaller, dimmer.

There was little Max could do. He knew he was sailing straight. But it was as if the bay were extending itself in front of him, adding distance between his boat and his destination. He turned around but saw no sign of the bay he'd left, the forest of his lean-to. He saw nothing of his neighborhood at all. There was only a moon overhead and the rough shimmer on the waves. He had no choice but to continue traveling along his present course, for going any other way made no sense at all.

He hoped that somewhere in the night the bay would become rational again and the city would reappear. He would have to tell his father about this strange elastic stretching of the bay! But soon the city was disappearing altogether. For a while it was no more than a twinkle of dwindling lights, and shortly thereafter, it was gone. There was no sign of land in any direction. He didn't want to admit it to himself, but some part of Max acknowledged that in all likelihood, he'd left the bay altogether, and was now in the open sea.

Before Max was even tired, the moon had fallen through the water and the sun had risen to replace it. He'd sailed all night without sleep and was too bewildered to think about rest. Max continued sailing north-northwest, but now saw nothing anywhere at all. Not a fish, not a bird. The wind had slackened and the sea grew wider and broader and more interminable and boring. By his rough calculations he had to be at least seven million miles from where he left off.

Finally, as the sun climbed higher, he was tired enough to sleep. He pulled in the sail, tied it to the mast, rigged the rudder so it would remain true, and fell asleep.

When he awoke, it was night again. The same moon he'd left just hours ago was back. Max sailed through the night, falling asleep again not long after. He felt weak; it had been so long since he'd eaten.

With a shock of recognition, Max was finally sure he was in the open ocean. His compass did not seem to be working, and he hadn't seen any sign of land or life in days. Where was he going? How long could he survive like this? His mind followed a dozen terrible paths until he realized, with some comfort, that there was nothing he could do, really, about his situation. He could only sail straight and hope for the best.

The following morning brought about the longest day Max had ever known. The length of a day! Alone in his boat, the straight line of ocean unbroken on any side, every minute was a day, one hour was longer than any life ever lived.

His mind ran out of things to think about. He thought of everything he'd ever thought of by midday and then could only start over. He counted all the states: CA, CO, NV, OR, WA, ID, SD, ND, WY, NE, IL, IN, IA, MI, WI, KS, MT... He was stumped at twenty-four. Even so, a record for him. He named all of his classmates, dividing them into the ones he knew, the ones he tolerated, the ones he didn't know and those he would punch in the head if he had the chance. He named the families on his street, on the next street. He named all of his teachers, past and present, and all of the members of that year's Brazilian Olympic soccer team.

He named all of his uncles and aunts. Uncles Stuart, Grant, Scotty, Wash and Jeff, Aunts Isabelle, Paulina, Lucy, Juliet. The last time he'd seen them all was at that strange reunion. Where had it been? In some log cabin somewhere, in Colorado or near Colorado. It was on a hill, and the cabin was cramped with people, the smell of pine and soup and venison, and so much beer, so much drinking all the time. There was fishing, and there were games of

Twister, and runs through the woods, and then, when it rained, long cramped days and nights in the too-small cabin. Sounds coming from all the rooms, tiny tantrums a dozen a day, so many moods and slights and silences and bursts of almost-violence. And because there weren't enough beds, almost everyone slept in one room, by the stove, limbs overlapping, so many sounds. It had been fun, and then frightening, and then fun, and finally, thankfully, it was over. He'd slept all twelve hours home in the car.

He loosened a nail on the boat's bench and removed it. He used it to count the hours (as close as he could approximate) as they passed, marking them as a prisoner would. On the outer rim of the boat he carved his name as big as he could, so any fish or whales or passing ships would know who commanded this vessel: MAX, it said, in a way both tidy and slightly menacing.

He tried to draw a map of the world on the boat floor, then drew kodiak bears — all he could draw was a kodiak bear; his father, a decent draftsman, had taught him this one skill — and while he was drawing his third kodiak bear, this one eating his own paw, Max decided to calculate exactly how long it had been since his father left.

The timeline was becoming blurry in his mind. Was it three years ago? That was what he'd been saying when people asked, but had he been saying it so long that it was now four years ago? The order of events was unclear.

He had memories of his father and Gary together. But was that even possible? No, that was impossible. And the man before Gary, the white-haired man named Peter.

When did *he* come and go? Would it have been possible that all these men knew each other?

Now Max was getting confused. Of course it wasn't possible for them to all know each other. There had been a linear sequence of events. First there was his father. Then his father was gone for a business trip — one month, then two, then it wasn't a business trip anymore. He was simply gone, and soon had gotten the place in the city. Then there was quiet. Then he was back for that one loud week, then gone again. Then quiet again, for what seemed like a year. Then the white-haired Peter. Who was he again? He was too old. He once brought Max a plant, a fern, for a present. Max put it on the window sill and later made sure it "fell" into the garden below. Then Peter was gone... though he came back that one late night and woke everyone up with his singing and begging. Right? That was Peter.

Then came Gary. But what about the other-other man, the man who came to the door a few times last year? His mother had gone with him in his car, a small convertible the color of ash... Max had asked Claire about that man, but she told Max he was only someone from his mother's work; they had to go to a working dinner, she told him. Max was sure there was more to it than that, but there were secrets between Claire and his mother. Too many.

Max sailed in and out of days and nights. He endured blustery winds, cruel winds, chattering winds, and warm blanketing breezes. There were waves like dragons and waves like sparrows. There was rain but mostly there was sun, the terribly unimaginative sun, doing the same things day in and day out. There were occasional sightings of birds and fish and flies, but nothing Max could reach or much less eat. He had not had a morsel of anything in what seemed like weeks and it was causing a churning ache within him that felt as if his organs were feeding on each other for sustenance.

CHAPTER XV

But one day he saw something. A green blot on the horizon, no bigger than a caterpillar. Half-crazed and untrusting of his eyes, he thought little of it. He went to sleep again.

When he awoke, the caterpillar had become an island. It towered above him — a rocky beach beneath massive cliffs, green hills above. The island seemed strangely alive everywhere, vibrating with color and sound.

By the time he reached the shore, it was night and the island had gone black. It was a good deal less welcoming now, as a silhouette against a gunmetal sky, but there was something high in the hills that beckoned him. An orange glow between the trees high above the shore.

As soon as he felt he was able, Max jumped out and into the water. He thought it would be at least waist-deep, but it was far deeper than that. His feet could not reach the floor and he was quickly swallowed in the foam, the white. And the cold! The water was colder than he thought possible; it knocked the wind out of him.

He held the rope that held the boat, and tried to dog-paddle shoreward. He thought for a moment he would have to let go of the rope, lest he drown. But just as his head dropped below the surface and the boat tugged against his grip, his feet found the sand below, and he stood. He would not die this night and he considered this, on balance, a good thing.

Max stumbled forth, soaked and exhausted. He dragged the boat onto the beach, placed a group of large stones around it, and tied its lead to the biggest tree he could find. When he was finished, he collapsed and lay down, his cheek to the cold sand. When he felt rested, he rose again, but found he could barely stand. He was tired and hungry and leaden; the weight of his fur when wet surprised him. He considered taking off his wolf suit, but he knew if he did he'd be even colder. The wind was bracing and he knew that his only chance at warmth — of survival — would be to climb the cliffs and find his way to the fire he'd seen from the sea.

So this is what he did.

The cliffs were jagged but dependable. He climbed to the top in under an hour and rested at the summit. While heaving and looking down — he was easily two hundred feet up — he heard the sounds coming from the island's interior: crunching and crashing, whooping and howling, the crackle of a gigantic fire. Only in his depleted and desperate state would Max have considered his best option to be to run, stumble, and crawl through the densest and wildest kind of jungle toward the sounds of what seemed to be some kind of riot.

But this is what he did.

He walked for hours. He slashed his way through the undergrowth, ducking under grasping, luminescent ferns and slithering between the barbed and crosshatched vines. He waded through narrow creeks — the water strangely hot — and climbed over boulders covered with a red and delicate moss that clung to the stone like embroidery. The landscape was sometimes familiar — there were trees, there was dirt, there were rocks — but then again, very odd: the earth seemed to be striped in brown and yellow, like peanut butter and cinnamon after the first twirl of a mixing spoon. There were holes, perfect holes, cut widthwise in the trunks of most of the trees.

After some time his fur, at least above his shins, was dry, and he was warmer, but he was so tired he was dreaming on his feet. Again and again he would shudder awake and find that he'd been walking while asleep.

He was kept going, and on track, by the increasing volume of the chaos in the center of the island. It was such a strange mix of sounds — destruction, calamity, but then what seemed to be laughing.

CHAPTER XVI

And then, when he reached the top of a long high hill, he saw the fire, huge and snapping at the black sky. Most of it was obscured by a giant boulder in his line of vision, but the fire's size was clear: it licked the surrounding trees orange and blotted out the stars above. It was intentional, it had a center and a purpose.

Then movement. He saw something.

First there was just a blur. Some kind of creature shooting through the trees, a rushing figure silhouetted by the red fire beyond. It could have been a bear, he thought, but the animal seemed to be running upright, on two feet.

Max dropped to his knees, holding his breath.

Again a figure darted between the trees. This one was the same size as the previous creature, but Max would have sworn he'd seen a beak. It seemed to Max's tired eyes that a giant rooster, twelve feet tall, had just run across his field of vision.

Max had half a mind to turn and run — for what good could come of engaging beasts of that size near a fire of that strength? — but he couldn't leave just yet. The warmth of the blaze had awakened him, and he had to know what was happening down there.

He dropped to his stomach, snaking closer. He only needed to make his way up the boulder between himself and the fire to see what was happening below. He was making his way commando-style, when a cat, a simple orange house cat but for its size — it was only four or five inches high — stepped in front of him and hissed.

Max had never encountered a four-inch-high cat before, so he had no plan of action. He hissed back at the cat and it stopped, tilted its head, and looked at him quizzically. It then sat on its hind legs, lifted a tiny paw, and began grooming itself.

Max heard more crashing, the sounds of splintering wood, but he saw nothing. He was sad to leave the tiny cat, but figured he would see more of its kind on the island, and by the time he did, he would have worked out what to do with one.

So he skulked forward, again toward the fire. He wanted the warmth it promised, and he wanted whatever food might have been roasted on it, and he wanted more than anything else to find out just what was going on.

A hundred yards more and he knew.

CHAPTER XVII

Sort of. That is, he saw what he saw but couldn't believe any of it. He saw animals. Animals? Creatures of some kind. Huge and fast. He thought they might be an oversized kind of human covered in fur but they were bigger than that, hairier than that. They were ten or twelve feet tall, four hundred pounds each or more. Max knew his animal kingdom, but he had no name for these beasts. From behind they resembled bears, but they were larger than bears, their heads far bigger, and they were quicker than bears or anything so large. Their movements were nimble, deft — they had the quickness of deer or small monkeys. And they all looked different, as humans do — one had a long broken horn on its nose; another had a wide flat face, stringy hair, and pleading eyes; another seemed like a cross between a boy and a goat. And another—

It *had* been a giant rooster. This was the weirdest one by far. Max slapped himself, making sure he was awake.

He was awake, and there was a giant rooster before him, no more than twenty yards away, in the full glow of the raging fire. It was at once comical — it looked like a giant man in a rooster suit, standing upright — and powerful and menacing.

The rooster creature seemed frustrated, staring at another creature, this one of similar height and heft, but with a different shape. This one had a mop of reddish hair and a leonine face, with a large rhino-like horn extending from its nose. It looked female, if that was possible for such an ugly thing. She was in the middle of destroying something, beating a large nest with a log. In her enthusiasm and abandon, she looked like a kid destroying a sand castle.

And this seemed to be greatly upsetting the rooster.

Soon Max could see a pattern to what the beasts were doing. It looked like they'd come upon some kind of settlement, full of great round nests — each made of huge sticks and logs and every one of them bigger than a car — and they had decided to destroy them. They were systematically wrecking them all. They ripped the nests open, they jumped from trees into them, they tossed each other into the nest-walls which collapsed instantly from the force.

Max was about to turn and run the other way — there didn't seem to be much point in staying so close to such destructive, borderline maniacal beasts — when he heard (could it be?) a word.

There was, he was almost sure, a word: "Go!"

He would have never expected them to speak, but he was sure he'd heard the word *Go*. And just as he was repeating the sound in his mind, turning it over, analyzing it, the creature closest to him spoke a full sentence:

"Is it twisted?"

This one was standing, showing his back to another, who was sitting at his feet. They seemed to have fallen through the wall of one of the huts, and the first was asking for help, assessing possible injuries to his spine.

"Yeah, it's kind of twisted," said the second.

The two gathered themselves up and ran off.

Max squatted down again, determined to watch a bit longer, to try and parse what was happening and why.

One creature seemed to be leading the melee. He had a big round face, sharp horns like a viking's and dark bags under his eyes. He was getting ready to run toward one of the nests when the rooster-looking creature approached him and put his hand — it wasn't a wing; he seemed to have hands and claws — on his shoulder.

"Carol, can I speak to you for a second?"

Max was astounded. Had that sentence just been uttered? It was said with such casual sophistication that his conception of the creatures was exploded. They weren't just grunting monsters: they spoke like people.

"Not now, Douglas," the big one, Carol, said, and moved the rooster to one side. Then Carol got a running start and barreled into the side of one of the nests, knocking it to splinters.

Meanwhile, a giant bull-like creature was running into various walls at even greater speed. He seemed disconnected, though, not seeking out anyone's approval or interacting in any meaningful way.

"Good job," Max said to him.

The bull stared at Max, but said nothing. Then he turned away, moving like a ship, and lumbered off.

Max could now see that a smaller creature was upset about all the activity. This one resembled a goat, standing upright and with white-grey fur. He was the shortest and thinnest of the creatures by far, closer to Max's size than the others. He was yelling "Stop!" and "Why are you doing this?" and in between whimpering in a way Max thought kind of unappealing. He was pointedly ignored by the rest of the beasts.

DOU GLAS

Max watched and listened until he had a sense of all of their names and how they fit into what he had begun to understand was some kind of family.

There was the rooster. His name was Douglas. He seemed logical and even-tempered, and didn't appreciate the way that Carol was trying to amuse himself and the others.

CAROL

Carol, the main instigator and heartiest of the destroyers, was the biggest, the strongest, the loudest. His fur bore horizontal stripes on his torso like some kind of sweater, and his claws were huge and cleaver-sharp.

There was the female one with the horn and the red mop of hair. Her name was Judith, and she had a sharp, pokey voice and a harsh cackle for a laugh.

JUDITH

Max was having trouble keeping them straight, so using his Kodiak-drawing skills, he started sketching in the dirt under him, attaching names to his crude renderings.

Ira was the bulb-nosed one, and he seemed to be always close to Judith. Max guessed they might even be a couple, though a strange one. He had a sad sort of aura and poor posture.

IRA

There was the goat-shaped one, Alexander, with a snarl for a face and pin-thin legs. He was just a little bigger than Max.

ALEX.

And then there was the bull. He was gigantic, maybe thirteen feet high, and seemed built entirely of muscle and stone. He hadn't said a word yet.

That made six. Six of the beasts overall. Wait. No, seven. There was one who didn't seem to be participating in the destruction. She had a melancholy face and was sitting off by herself, on a boulder overlooking the chaos. With long straw-brown hair and little ears poking through, she had sweet, gentle eyes and fangs that despite their size (about as big as Max's hands) seemed kind of cute.

BULL

Now Carol, the biggest one, was tossing Alexander, the goat, high into the air. He would toss him twenty or thirty feet, then catch him and toss him higher. It looked dangerous and crazy and Max very much wanted

KATHERINE

to be the goat. He wanted to be thrown, he wanted to fly, he wanted to knock things down.

After the fourth toss, Carol threw Alexander straight into one of the nests. Alexander emerged from the wreckage laughing what seemed to be a fake laugh, as if he hadn't enjoyed it at all but wanted to seem up for anything.

Max was more intrigued every moment. The beasts jumped from trees into the nests, they tossed each other into piles, they rolled boulders into the remains of the structures. It was just about the best mayhem Max had ever seen.

But soon there was a lull in the action. One by one the beasts seemed to have quit their destruction. They sat down, scratching themselves and nursing small wounds.

"I'm bored," one of them said.

"Me too," said another.

The leader, the one named Carol, wasn't happy to let it die. "C'mon!" he roared. "Let's finish this!"

There was no answer from the rest of them. The bulb-nosed one sat down. Carol jogged over to him — they really were agile things, these creatures.

"Ira," he said to the bulb-nosed one, "we're not done yet. The job isn't complete."

"But I'm so tired!" Ira said. "And uninspired."

"Hey, don't think you can rhyme your way out of this. Uninspired? How's that possible?" Carol turned to address the rest of the creatures. "C'mon, isn't this fun? Who's gonna really go crazy with me?"

No one responded. Carol jumped from beast to beast,

trying to create some excitement. When he approached Douglas, Douglas questioned the entire endeavor. "Carol, why are we doing this in the first place?" he asked.

A quick cloud came over Carol's face. His teeth — a hundred of them, each as big as Max's hand — were bared in something between a smile and a show of force.

"Douglas, I don't have to tell you, do I? We all know why they need to go. They weren't good enough. You heard Katherine. She said it was time— "

"That's not what I meant," someone said. It was the almost-cute beast on the rock. This must be Katherine, Max thought.

"We all heard what you said," Carol growled. "You said it was all wrong, that everything we'd made was cruddy and needed to be torn down."

Katherine sighed, exasperated. "I said nothing of the sort. You mangle everything I say."

Carol decided to ignore her. "All I need to know now is if there's anyone on this island who's brave and creative and wild enough to help finish this job. Is there anyone up to it?"

No one responded.

"Anyone?"

CHAPTER XVIII

Something clicked in Max. His thoughts lined up, his plan was orderly and clear. He needed to be that someone.

Max dashed down the hill and through the legs of Douglas and Ira, his face a knot of determination. The creatures towered over him, and outweighed him by thousands of pounds.

"Whoa, what's that?" Ira said, alarmed.

"Look at his little legs!" Judith squealed.

"What's he doing?" Douglas asked.

Max intended to show them. He took a torch from the fire and threw it onto one of the remaining roofs in the settlement. With a roar and a whoosh, the roof went up in flames.

The beasts cheered.

Max took another torch and threw it. He was aiming for another roof but it went too far; it sailed up into a tree, where it caught fire. The whole tree exploded into triumphant flame, as if soaked in kerosene.

The creatures cheered louder.

Max was aghast at the flaming tree but couldn't do anything to extinguish it, or the enthusiasm of the creatures. They'd taken Max's cue and now were throwing torches onto everything — roofs, trees, themselves.

One creature, the rooster-looking one named Douglas, was suddenly on fire. He wailed until he jumped into a nearby stream, dousing himself and then giggling wildly.

Whoosh! Another tree went up in flames. And another. Soon Carol was climbing one of the trees, as the flames went higher. He shook the low boughs and sent sparks showering down on them all.

The heat was incredible, and it made Max feel stronger than he'd ever felt. Max danced below the flames, thrilled with the chaos.

"Burn them all!" Carol said. "Burn the trees!"

And soon there were dozens on fire. The whole forest was on fire.

For a moment Max panicked, worried that he had started a fire that would consume the whole island. But after some examination, he could see that the forest was not endless. It ran alongside a stream on one side and abutted a treeless hill on the other. The fire would burn through this small forest and end, he hoped.

In the meantime, the scene was spectacular. The sky was orange. Fire rained down. Birds left their nests and rose from the flames like embers, twisting and leaping into the sky. And Max had started it all.

"Yes!" Carol yelled. "Yes, yes! Knock them all down!" he said, and then ran headlong into one of the remaining nests. It popped open like a jack-in-the-box. Carol emerged grinning, and found Max grinning back at him.

Together they picked up a long log and ran together at another nest, laying waste to it. Max had never destroyed so much so well and so quickly. He followed Carol to one of the last nests and he and Carol both lifted large sticks over their heads, about to crush it with simultaneous blows.

"Hey new guy!" Judith snapped. "Don't touch that one."

Max hesitated.

"What?" Carol took exception to this command and shook his head at Max, dismissing the warning. "No, keep going. Knock it down."

Judith turned to Max with a look of great severity: "Don't you dare."

Max stood between the two of them, unsure who to obey, who to defy.

"Don't lay a finger on it," she warned.

With a laugh, Carol kicked his immense foot into the structure, reducing it to splinters. "There," he said. "Not a finger."

Max had to laugh. That was pretty good. He watched as Carol, his comrade-in-arms, ran over to the other side of the clearing, looking for anything left standing.

Max looked too. But as far as he could see, there was nothing left to destroy. The trees, the few that still stood, were charred and their branches had been stripped or brought down. Max stood in the middle of a desolate grey plain. The nests were no more. He started to walk toward Carol, to congratulate him on the completeness of their wreckage, when Douglas appeared in front of Max, blocking his path.

"What are you doing here?" he asked.

"What? I'm just helping," Max said.

"Then why are you burning and smashing our houses?"

"These are your houses?" This was news to Max. He'd assumed they were destroying some enemy encampment. "Why are *you* smashing them?"

"*I'm* not, actually. You're not very observant for someone swinging that big stick around."

Max dropped the stick.

"Wait," Alexander said, standing in the wreckage, alone and teary-eyed, like a child lost at the mall. "Where will we sleep tonight?"

Suddenly there seemed to be a realization spreading throughout the beasts.

"I was trying to tell you all that," Douglas said.

"Well don't blame me," Judith said.

"Why not?" Douglas said, "you were wrecking as much as anyone else. You wrecked everything but your own nest."

"Sure, but I didn't enjoy it," she said. "And anyway, it wasn't my fault."

Douglas was shaking his head. "Then whose fault is it?"

Judith looked around for a moment and settled, rather happily, on Max.

"The new guy!" she said. "He's the one who got every-one riled up. And the fire was his thing, too."

Douglas paused thoughtfully, then nodded, acknowl-edging the truth in this. Judith, feeling empowered, pointed more forcefully.

"And you know what I say you do with a problem? Eat it!" she said, and started toward Max.

"Yeah," Alexander said, "he's the problem!"

Now Judith and Alexander were making their way to Max. Ira hadn't been paying attention.

"What are you guys doing?" he asked.

"Oh, we were just gonna eat that," Judith said, point-ing to Max, as if picking out a lobster at a restaurant.

"Okay," Ira said, shrugging and beginning to drool.

Max was very quickly in the shadow of the three of them, and soon Douglas and the bull had joined the throng, and it was very dark and warm with beast-sweat. Max backed up until he found himself against a mess of sticks and mud where a home used to be. There was no es-cape. The beasts seemed to notice this, too, and were grin-ning. Max looked from one to the other, as the four of them grew closer.

"He looks tasty," Ira said.

"Does he?" Judith said, "I don't know. I'm thinking gamey."

"Gamey?" Douglas mused. "Really? I say succulent."

"Succulent?" Judith said. "I don't know. I'll give you tasty, but not *succulent*."

Alexander chimed in: "All I know is I'm getting hun-grier just looking at him."

"He's an ugly bugger, though, isn't he?" Judith said.

"Close your eyes then. I'll feed him to you," Ira said.

"Oh, that's so romantic!" she said.

"Hold on!" a voice yelled from across the camp. It was Carol. Max felt some relief, and yet the creatures were still closing in on Max. It was too late to stop them. Max could feel their hot wet breath on his face, he could see their enormous teeth, each incisor as big as his foot. They could kill him long before Carol would have time to intervene.

Again the big one sent his voice from afar. "Wait!"

Ira licked his lips. The bull snorted, his hands reaching.

Max knew Carol couldn't save him in time. He had to save himself — somehow. He arched his back and with a voice far louder and more commanding than he ever expected, he roared, "Be still!"

CHAPTER XIX

The beasts stopped. They stopped moving, stopped talk-ing, stopped raising their arms to claw Max to death, stopped salivating profusely. Max couldn't believe it. He didn't know what to do next.

"Why?" said Judith. "Why should we stop?"

This was a tricky question, Max knew. If *he* were about to bite into, say, a strawberry, and it told him to stop, he too would want a good explanation.

"Because... Uh... Because..." he mumbled.

The beasts stared, waiting, blowing roughly through their nostrils. Max knew he had to come up with some-thing immediately, and to his surprise, he did. "Because," he said, "I heard about this one time that they weren't still and they..."

"Who?" said Judith. "Who wasn't still?"

Now Carol arrived, standing behind the others. He had been impressed with Max before, but now he seemed in awe of this small creature's presence and power.

"Um… The hammers," Max explained, making it up as he went along, "they were huge ones and they didn't know how to be still. They were *crazy*. They were always shaking and running around and they never stopped to see what was right in front of them. So this one time the hammers were storming down the mountainside and they couldn't even see that someone was coming up to *help* them. And you know what happened?"

The beasts, enthralled, shook their heads.

"They ran right over him and *killed* him," Max said.

There were a few gasps, but there were also a few sounds that said "Well, what *else* would they do?"

"And the thing is," Max added, "he *liked* them. He was there to *help*."

"Who was he?" asked Douglas.

"Who was who?" Max said.

"The guy coming up the hill," Douglas said.

"He was…" And again Max fumbled in the velvet darkness of his mind and found, impossibly, a gem. "He was their king," Max answered.

Max had never told a more bizarre story, but the creatures were just floored by it.

Carol stepped forward. "Do *you* like *us*?"

This was a tough question. Max wasn't sure that he liked any of them, given they were, moments earlier, about to devour his flesh and brains. But in the interest of self-preservation, and because he had been liking them a lot when they were all breaking things and lighting trees on fire, he said, "Yeah. I like you."

Ira cleared his throat and said, with a hope-filled catch in his voice, "Are you *our* king?"

Max had rarely had to do so much bluffing in his life. "Sure. Yeah," he said. "I think so."

A ripple of excitement spread through the beasts.

"Wow, he's the king," Ira said, now seeming very happy.

"Yeah," Douglas said. "Looks like he is."

"Why is *he* the king?" Alexander said, full of sarcasm. "*He's* not a king. If *he* can be king, *I* could be king."

Thankfully, as usual, all the other creatures ignored the goat.

"He's very small," noted Judith.

"Maybe that's why he'll be good," suggested Ira. "That way he can fit in small places."

Douglas stepped forward, as if he'd just thought of a stumper of a question that might decide it all: "Were you king where you came from?"

Max was getting good at the fibbing, so this one was easy. "Yeah, I was. King Max. For twenty years," he said.

A quick happy murmur spread through the creatures.

"Are you going to make this a better place?" Ira asked.

"Sure," Max said.

"Because it's screwed up, let me tell you," Judith blurted.

"Quiet, Judith," Carol said.

"No, really, I could tell you stories…" she continued.

"Judith, stop," Carol snapped.

But she wasn't finished: "All I'm saying is that if we're gonna have a king, he might as well solve all our problems. It's the least he can do, after knocking over all our houses."

"Judith, of course he's here to fix everything," Douglas said. "Why else would a king be a king and a king be here?" He turned to Max. "Right, King?"

"Uh, sure," Max said.

Carol smiled. "Well, that settles it then. He's our king!" They all moved in to hug Max.

"Sorry we were gonna eat you," Douglas said.

"We didn't know you were king," Ira said.

"If we'd known you were the king, we almost definitely wouldn't have tried to eat you," Judith added, then laughed in a sudden, mirthless trill. She lowered her voice to a confessional tone. "We just got caught up in the moment."

CHAPTER XX

Max was swept up and lifted high in the air and finally set down on the shoulders of the Bull. The Bull — that seemed to be his name — followed Carol into a cave under an enormous tree. Inside the cave, there were two torches illuminating a golden oval of a room.

The Bull put Max down and rooted around in a small pile of rubble on the ground. He soon retrieved a scepter, copper-colored and bejeweled, and gave it to Max. Max inspected it reverently. It was heavy, but not too heavy. It was perfect, with a hand-carved handle and a crystal orb at the top.

The Bull continued to dig through the rubble. Curious, Max peered around the Bull and saw that it wasn't a pile of sticks and rocks but a pile of what looked to be bones. They were yellowed and broken, the remains of what seemed like a dozen different creatures. Twisted and spotted skulls and ribs in sizes and shapes Max had never seen in any book or museum.

"Aha!" Carol bellowed. "There it is."

Max looked up to see that the Bull had pulled a crown from the heap. It was golden, rough-hewn, and the Bull turned to place the crown on Max's head. Max pulled away.

"Wait," he said, pointing to the pile of bones. "Are those… other kings?"

The Bull glanced quickly to Carol with a look of mild concern.

"No, no!" Carol said, chuckling. "Those were there before we got here. We've never even seen them before."

Max was unconvinced.

"What are those, anyway?" Carol asked the Bull.

The Bull shrugged elaborately.

Then Carol and the Bull did a quick jig atop the bones, reducing them to dust.

"See?" Carol said, grinning, his eyes nervous and alight. "Nothing to worry about. Just all this dust." He turned to the Bull. "Make sure you dust in here next time!"

Sensing Max's apprehension, Carol stepped forward and spoke with great solemnity. "I promise you have nothing to worry about, Max. You're the king. And nothing bad can happen to the king. Especially a good king. I can already tell you'll be a truly great king."

Max looked into Carol's eyes, each of them as big as a volleyball. They were the warmest brown and green, and seemed sincere.

"But what do I have to do?" Max asked.

"Do? Anything you want to do," Carol said.

"And what do *you* have to do?" Max asked.

"Anything you want us to do," Carol said. He answered so quickly that Max was convinced.

"Then okay," Max said.

Max lowered his head to receive his crown. Carol gently placed it on Max's head. It was heavy, made of something like iron, and the metal was cool on his forehead. But the crown fit, and Max smiled. Carol stood back and looked at him, nodding as if everything had finally fallen into place.

The Bull lifted Max and placed him on his shoulder, and as they made their way out of the tunnel, there were deafening cheers from the rest of the beasts. The Bull paraded Max around the forest, as everyone whooped and danced in a very ugly — drool and mucus spraying left and right — but celebratory kind of way. After a few minutes, the Bull placed Max atop a grassy knoll, and the beasts gathered around, looking up to him expectantly. Max realized he was supposed to say something, so he said the only thing he could think of:

"Let the wild rumpus begin!"

CHAPTER XXI

The beasts cheered. Then they waited for Max to tell them what to do. They knew how to rumpus, but they wanted to make sure they did it to the pleasing of their king.

Max shimmied down the Bull's torso and began to spin around like a dervish. "Do what I do!" he demanded.

And they did. The beasts were terrible dervishes, clumsy and slow at spinning, but this made it all more entertaining for Max. He watched and laughed as they spun themselves into a mass of dizzy fur and feet, each of them crumpling to the ground.

For the next five or six hours, Max thought of every fun thing he could possibly think of, and he made sure all the beasts did these things with him.

He sat on Ira's back and made him act like a horse (though Ira had never heard of a horse). He lined them all up like dominoes and ordered them to knock each other over. He made them assemble themselves into a giant pyramid, and he climbed on the top and deliberately caused the pyramid to fall. The beasts were extraordinary diggers, so Max made them dig dozens of holes, huge holes, for no reason at all. Then it was back to knocking down trees — the ten or twelve that remained. It was Max's task to think of as many ways as possible to knock them down, and to do it as loudly as possible.

Next Max thought it would be good to run up to the closest hill and roll down like giant furry earth balls. So he ran and the beasts followed him up the hill. At the top, he demonstrated how it should be done. He somersaulted down the grassy hill and when he was finished, he saw that Douglas and Alexander had already followed his lead and were rolling down after him. But their speed was about triple his, and they were headed directly for him.

He jumped out of the way just in time, and made a mental note to remind them to be more careful next time they rolled down the hill with him nearby. But just as he was dusting himself off, Carol and Judith barreled down the hill even faster than their predecessors, again directly toward Max. Again he had to jump out of the way, but this time his foot was clipped by the Judith-ball, and he yowled in pain.

"What's the matter?" she asked, unspooling herself at the bottom of the hill.

"You rolled over my foot!" he said.

Judith looked at him blankly. "And?"

"You shouldn't do that!" Max said.

Judith gave him a look like he'd just said by far the most insane thing. Max had the momentary thought that he should bash her over the head with a stick or rock. He looked around for something that would do the job. But before he could, Carol stepped in.

"Judith, did you roll over the king's foot?" Carol asked.

"I don't know what I did," she replied dryly. "I have no memory of any of it. Wait, where am I?"

"You know very well what you did," Carol said, stepping closer to her. "And if you do that again, I swear I'll eat your head."

Max, flattered that Carol would come to his defense but startled by the threat, patted Carol on the arm. "That's okay, Carol. But thanks."

Judith was aghast. "'Thanks?' You say 'thanks' for threatening to eat my head? *That's* what you're thanking him for? What kind of king thanks someone for threatening to eat one of his subject's heads?"

While Max tried to concoct a response, Ira was trying to figure out the king's point of view.

"So we should try *not* to run over your foot when we turn ourselves into balls, but then if we *do* run over you, we get our heads eaten?"

"Yes," Carol said, relieved that someone had finally figured out the obvious.

"No!" Max wailed. "No. There won't be any running over feet, and no eating of heads. No eating any part of each other. That's just the main rule, okay?"

"But what if we *want* to?" Douglas asked.

"What do you mean?" Max asked.

"I mean, we shouldn't eat heads, and that makes sense. But what if we find ourselves in a position where we really *want* to eat someone's head or maybe arm?"

Again there was a wide murmur of approval over this worthy question.

Max was having a hard time controlling his exasperation. He took a number of deep breaths and explained, as slowly and carefully as he could, the rules under which he wanted his subjects to live. There would be no eating of each other under any circumstances — even if they wanted to — and no running over each other in any way at all, and no...

Alexander interrupted. "But what if someone's head *falls* off? That sometimes happens. Can we eat it then?" he asked, eliciting a chorus of approving murmurs.

"No eating at all!" Max roared. "No eating any part of each other under any circumstances. Never. Not even if a head pops off."

Max wanted to stop talking and start howling, so he ran away, leading everyone to the edge of the island.

"C'mon!" he said, and they all followed.

He did somersaults along the way, and they did them, too. He skipped, and they skipped, too — or tried to. He made machine-gun sounds, and they did their best. And soon they were at what must have been the highest point on the island, a cliff overlooking the ocean, hundreds of feet over the water. When they had all joined him at the edge of the cliff, Max knew there was nothing more appropriate to do than howl.

So Max howled. The beasts howled, too, louder and more convincingly than Max, but he didn't mind. Nothing could improve upon the moment or spoil it. Max howled and howled and felt more like himself — part wind and part wolf — than he ever had before.

Nothing could spoil the moment, not even when Alexander joined the group, pushing everyone from behind and nearly killing Max. When Alexander bumped the group, the bumping continued until someone bumped hard into Max, and suddenly there was no ground beneath him. He looked down for a split second and saw only the white mess of the sea meeting the chalky rocks below. But just when Max realized that he was in the air, that he was about to fall four hundred feet into the ocean, he was pulled back and put on solid earth. It had been Carol. He was caught just in time and quickly put back on solid ground. Max was too shocked, too disbelieving, to even register how close he'd just come to disappearing from the world of the living. Instead, he planted his feet wide and howled at the sea that had been robbed of his flesh.

The rest of the beasts joined in. They howled loudly, crazily. They howled until they were hoarse. When they were unable to howl any more, Max heard a giggling coming from the side of the group.

He turned to see Katherine, the stringy-haired one, smiling at him in a smirky, knowing sort of way.

"What?" he asked.

"Nothing," she said.

Her voice was that of a scruffy young woman. It was low and gravelly, but appealing, even musical.

Max looked at her, not understanding. He was intimidated by her smirk. "What?"

"Nothing. You're having fun," she said.

"What does that mean?" Max asked.

"Nothing," she said.

"Nothing?" Max asked.

"It means what it means," she said. "It's nice."

Just then Max heard a loud thump coming from the forest. He looked through the trees, what was left of them, to find Carol jumping high in the air, like a kangaroo but far more powerful. Each jump sent Carol forty feet in the air, and he landed each time with a thunderous thump.

Katherine seemed to know that Max wanted to follow Carol. "You go ahead," she said. "I'll see you later."

"Okay," Max said, and chased into the forest after Carol, trying to get his attention. "Hey!" he yelled. "Hey!"

Carol slowed down and finally stopped. Max caught up. Carol grinned, breathing heavily through his nostrils.

"You're a good jumper," Max said.

"Yeah, I know!" Carol said. "I'm better than you think. I'm even better than *I* think I am!"

Max had noticed a great straight branch above them, and had an idea. "Can you jump up into that tree and catch yourself with your teeth?"

Carol made a face. "Of course I can," he said.

He jumped up, about twenty feet high, with his great mouth open, and when he got to the branch overhead, he timed it wrong. Instead of gripping the branch with his teeth, he hit it with his nose, and then fell to the ground awkwardly. The earth shook.

"Ow," he said.

Max was about to apologize and call off the experiment, but Carol was determined to do what Max had asked. He jumped again, growling on the way up, and this time caught the branch with his teeth. He hung from the branch, and looked down at Max proudly.

"Like this?" he asked. With the tree in his mouth, it sounded like "Ike gish?"

"Yeah, that's good," Max said, truly impressed.

Neither Max nor Carol was sure what to do next. Carol didn't want to jump down too soon, and Max was entertained by looking up at Carol, hanging there by his mouth.

"How's the weather up there?" Max asked.

"Fine," Carol tried to say.

Max laughed. "How much do you weigh?"

Carol tried to say "I don't know" but it came out in a barky muffle. Max laughed harder.

"How's it taste, that tree? Like pâté?" he said.

Carol had no idea what pâté was, but the ridiculous-sounding word caused him to laugh, and when he laughed, his teeth lost their grip, and he came plummeting down again. "Gow!" he yelled.

"Sorry," Max said. He felt awful about the idea, and about causing Carol to fall.

"No, no!" Carol said, doing a quick dance of pain, spinning around, holding his mouth and stomping his foot. "Not your fault. It was fun. It's just that something's caught in my tooth or something."

Douglas and Ira appeared. Douglas was dragging Ira by his feet, like a caveman with a bride, but backwards. Ira seemed exceedingly relaxed while being dragged, as if he were reclining on a hammock.

"Hey you guys," Carol said, standing in front of them. "Look at this. Do I have a piece of bark in here?"

Carol approached Douglas and Ira and opened his giant wet mouth, revealing two hundred or so huge, extremely sharp teeth in three concentric rows. Douglas leaned slightly away from Carol.

"I don't see anything," he said. "Clean as a whistle."

Carol looked down to Ira — who was still laying on the ground — searching for an answer.

"Nope. Clean as a whistle," Ira said, though there was no possible way Ira could see anything from his angle. He looked up to Max and extended his hand. "We haven't formally met. I'm Ira. I put the holes in the trees. Maybe you saw them? Or maybe not, I don't know. Anyway, it's what I do. It doesn't really help anyone, like you do. It's not crucial to the future of the world, like you are. And you probably already met Douglas. He's the one who gets the work done around here. Indispensible. Builder. Maker. Steadier of the unsteady— "

"Hey. Focus here," Carol said, pointing to his mouth again. "You gotta get closer."

"Heh heh. Looks good," Ira said. "All clear. Clean as a…"

"Yep, as a whistle," Douglas finished. The two of them seemed to be in a terrible hurry to get away from Carol's open mouth. "Come on, Ira, we have to go over there and… put some rocks in a pile."

Douglas led Ira away. Watching them leave, Carol's face hardened. Max saw all of this, concerned for Carol and the way Douglas and Ira didn't seem to trust Carol not to eat them. As Max was trying to figure out why Carol's good friends wouldn't want to get close to Carol's mouth, Carol turned to Max.

"Hey King, do I have something stuck in my teeth?" he said. He squatted down toward Max and opened his mouth.

Max peered into Carol's mouth. "I don't see anything."

Carol opened his mouth wider. "Maybe you need to look farther in?"

Max, before he could think better of it, put his knee on Carol's gum and ventured inside Carol's mouth.

"No, no. Even farther," Carol said.

Max went farther still, putting his knee onto the ridge of Carol's mouth. It was wet inside, and the smell was astounding. "Whoo. You've got bad breath!"

"Watch it," Carol said, laughing. "I could take your head off in one chomp."

And now Max could see the problem. There was a piece of bark, as big as a baseball mitt, stuck between two of Carol's back teeth. "It's a big piece," Max noted as he gently dislodged it. He emerged from Carol's mouth and presented the bark like a trophy fish.

Carol looked at it, amazed at its size. "Oh wow, thanks," he said. He held it in his hand for a while, staring at it. "Thanks, King. Really. I can't tell you how much that means to me," he said, and looked up to Max as if seeing him for the first time.

They were interrupted by Judith and the Bull and Alexander, who were running toward them, each of them blindfolded and carrying a dozen or so tiny cats. They were giggling like lunatics, and ran past Max and Carol and on down the hill, toward the remains of the forest. Max knew he had to follow, had to get himself a blindfold and some tiny cats, so follow he did.

CHAPTER XXII

There was a good deal more rumpusing done over the course of the night, all the way until the night paled into dawn and dawn tipped toward morning.

Max was becoming tired, at last, when he saw Katherine, the one who had given him the knowing smirk. She was alone, observing the mayhem from afar. Max watched her as she took everything in, processing it, a bit dismissively.

Then Max did the obvious thing: he ran up a tilted tree-trunk until he was above her, and then jumped onto her back, growling like a wolf.

Surprised, she stumbled back and fell to the ground, giggling. "I'm eating you for breakfast!" he yelled, as he pretended her stomach was oatmeal and his thumb was a spoon.

"Okay, okay," she sighed. "Just don't use any spices. I'm good enough as is."

This made Max laugh, and it caused in Katherine a

full-throated laugh, and the laughing aroused the attention of the rest of the beasts.

"Get over there and be social," Judith said, pushing Alexander directly onto Max and Katherine.

Now Max was on top of Katherine, and Alexander was on top of both of them, and because there seemed to be a pile in progress, Carol came running over and jumped atop them all. Seeing where this was going, Max ducked into the pile and found a safe pocket and covered his head. Judith soon jumped aboard, and Ira followed, and finally Douglas and the Bull. Each landing shook the earth.

When they had all arrived, Max found himself in a hollow at the bottom of the pile. It was dark and furry there, but he could imagine the look of the scrum from outside — probably twelve thousand pounds of hairy flesh, piled thirty feet high.

Groans and jokes ricocheted within.

"Somebody's leg is in my armpit."

"Who's drooling?"

"Drool? I thought that was ear-juice."

"Is someone tickling?"

"Carol, that's not funny. Don't."

"It *is* ear-juice. But it doesn't taste like mine."

The assemblage of bodies had created a network of Max-sized tunnels, so he began to crawl through. As he did, he felt like tickling everyone, so he did this, which turned up the volume on the laughing. It was deep, rumbling laughter, big vibrating laughter that shook the walls of the tunnels, changing them, and suddenly Max's leg was trapped under a pile of flab and fur. He pulled at it, to no avail. He began to get claustrophobic and more than a little nervous.

In the wall of bodies, a head suddenly turned, and a pair of huge eyes opened, like two headlights coming alive. Max looked up. It was Katherine.

"Hey," she said.

"Hey," Max said.

"Are you all right?"

"My foot's stuck."

With her free arm, she pushed someone's blubber off and reclaimed his foot for him.

"Now you owe me," she said.

"Okay," he said. He liked the idea of owing her.

She looked at Max, grinning for a moment. "Wow, I can't even *look* at you."

She closed her eyes tightly.

"Why?" Max asked.

Her eyes remained closed, a wide smile on her face. "I don't know. I guess you just seem *good.*"

"What do you mean?" he asked.

She opened one eye, just a sliver.

"Yeah, wow. It's almost unbearable."

Max didn't know what to say. Katherine opened her other eye just a bit now. "I'm getting used to it now," she said, squinting. "But it's like staring into the brightest light."

Max smiled. Was there something new about him that she was seeing? His stomach was shooting all over, splitting, oozing down his legs — he liked this creature, her bright eyes and raspy voice, so much that he couldn't control his interior.

"So why'd you come here?" she asked.

Max cleared his throat and thought of how he would explain it. "Well, I'm an explorer," he answered, trying to sound professional. "I explore."

"Oh, so no home or family?"

"No. Well. I mean..." This was a tough question, when Max really thought about it. What *had* become of his family? It seemed like months since he'd seen them. He tried to explain: "Well, I *had* a family but I—"

"You ate them?" she blurted, very excited.

"No!" Max gasped.

Katherine quickly backed away from her assumption. "Of course not! Who would do that?"

Max shrugged.

"So what *did* happen?" she asked.

Max wasn't sure how to explain what had happened. "I don't know," he started. "I did something. I mean, I think I did stuff to make them not like me anymore."

"So you left," she said, matter of factly. "That makes sense. Will you go back?"

"No. I can't," he said. "I caused permanent damage."

Katherine nodded gravely. "Permanent damage. Wow, that sounds serious." Just as quickly, she brightened into a bigger, toothier smile than before. "Well, now you're our king. Maybe you'll do a good job here."

Max really believed he could. "Yeah, I will," he said.

Just then, a body on top of Katherine shifted and seemed to put extra pressure on her head. She looked pained, her expression changing from a sleepy smile to one of great contortion.

"You okay?" Max said.

"Yeah, I'm used to that kind of thing," she said. "Well, good night," Katherine said, though her face was still squashed.

"Night," someone else said.

The beasts began to bid each other good night, and this turned into a hubbub of talk about the best parts of the rumpus.

Ira laughed. "Remember when we threw you, Judith? You were so beautiful."

"I'm most beautiful flying through the air, is that what you're saying? Was I beautiful when my head hit the rock?" She shrieked suddenly. "Hey, who's tickling?"

Ira got it next. "Yow! I think it's Carol. Is that you, Carol?"

Carol laughed. "Who, me? I would never— "

Judith snorted. "You haven't tickled in years, Carol. Is this the influence of the new king? Do we have more tickling to look forward to?"

"I told you, it's not me!" he said.

Then Judith shrieked again.

"Not there, Carol! I'm feeling vulnerable! No!"

As the rest of the pile calmed down and began to sleep and snore, Max crawled out of the pile-on to find fresh air. He settled on the edge of the fur mountain, putting his head on someone's leg. The sky was just beginning to change, the world pulsing in the gauzy pink light of dawn. There was debris everywhere, like a landscape after an earthquake, and Max felt very much at home.

CHAPTER XXIII

Max was still half-asleep, his eyes closed, when he realized he was bouncing. There was a gentle wind on his face, and the air was cool and crisp. He wasn't in the pile anymore, he figured — that smell had been strong, the air thick with sweaty fur. For a moment he feared he was back on the rolling sea, but when he opened his eyes he saw Carol's huge yellowed horns on either side of him, and realized he was on Carol's shoulders, being carried high above the earth.

"I didn't want to wake you up," Carol said. "But I'm glad you're up now. I want to show you something."

"Okay," Max said, starting to take everything in. On one side, the sea below was gold and glittering and endless, the sky a loud cobalt blue. All the colors here, on this island, from his perch atop Carol's shoulders, seemed triply bright and clear, vibrating.

Max reached atop his head. "Where's my crown?"

"You don't need the crown today," Carol explained. "I put it under the fire for you."

"Oh. Okay, thanks," Max said. Only after a moment did he realize he didn't know why his crown was under the fire. But it seemed to make sense to Carol, and he didn't want to question the custom.

They walked away from the cliff and through the forest, the undergrowth strange and new — ferns of orange, moss of yellow, vines of marbled white.

Max tried to take it all in, but he was exhausted. He couldn't have slept more than a few hours. And he was dirty. He smelled more of his own bodily secretions than ever before, and now his own smells had been amplified by the far more pungent odors of the beasts. He was not a lover of frequent cleanings of himself, but that morning he really had a hankering for a long hot shower.

"So how'd you get here?" Carol asked.

"Me? I sailed," Max said.

Carol whistled matter-of-factly. "Wow. You must be an extraordinary sailor."

"Yeah. But I don't like sailing much," Max said, suddenly remembering the boredom of it all, the ceaseless blinding glitter of the sun against the water.

"Yeah, me neither," Carol said excitedly. "Sailing is so boring! And there's nothing I hate more than being bored. If boredom was standing there in front of me right now" — he suddenly got louder — "I don't know if I could restrain myself. I'd probably just eat him!"

They both laughed at this. Max knew exactly what

Carol was talking about. Max had wanted to eat or kill so many boring things. Too many to mention.

Along the path, Max noticed a row of trees with holes bored in their trunks. The holes were tidy and round, about beast-height. Those must be Ira's, he thought.

"You were talking to Katherine last night," Carol said.

"The girl?" Max said. "Yeah, she's nice."

"Yeah, she is. She's sweet. She's… she's uh…" Carol did a fake sort of chuckle. "I bet she told you some things about me."

"No," he said, trying to remember. "No, she didn't say anything."

"She didn't? No? Nothing?" Carol let out a big laugh, entertained by this. "That's *fas*cinating."

Max and Carol continued down a winding path.

"Do you guys have parents?" Max asked.

"What do you mean?" Carol said.

"Like a mother and a father?"

Carol gave Max a puzzled look. "Of course we do. Everyone does. I just don't talk to mine because they're nuts."

They passed through some of the most bizarre landscapes Max had ever seen or dreamt. Hills that pulsated like gelatin, rivers that changed direction in midstream, small trees whose trunks, almost translucent, swallowed the sunlight and spun it into something pink and glassine.

"See, Max," Carol explained, as they left a forest and entered an area of grey-blue sand and tundra, "everything you can see is your kingdom. Everything on this island, pretty much. The trees with the holes in them are Ira's, of course, and some of the beach is kind of Katherine's, but otherwise it's all yours. And then there are parts of the forest where animals will definitely kill you, even though you're the king. They're just willful, just don't listen. But otherwise you're definitely the supreme ruler, and you can do whatever you want with stuff. And if anyone tells you otherwise, or tries to eat your limbs or face, just come to me and we'll crush them with rocks or something."

Max agreed.

They entered a wide flat area, rocky and desolate. Max knew this kind of landscape from Mr. Wisner's class. He climbed down from Carol's shoulders to inspect his surroundings.

"See that rock?" Max said, pointing to a shard of curved obsidian. "It used to be lava. And someday it'll be sand."

Carol was greatly impressed. "And what will it be after that?"

"I don't know…" Max said, stalling. "Maybe dust?"

"Dust, huh?" Carol said. "I thought you were going to say fire."

They walked for a while, hearing only the wind.

"Did you know the sun is going to die?" Max asked.

Max blurted it out, unplanned. But now that the question was out, he was happy it was. He figured that Carol might very well have an answer.

Carol stopped and looked down at Max and then up at the sun. "What? *That* sun?"

Max nodded.

"Die? How could it die?" Carol asked, truly flummoxed.

"I don't know. It'll go dark and maybe become a black hole."

"A black what? What are you talking about? Who told you something like that?"

"My teacher. Mr. Wisner."

"Mister Wis-who? That doesn't make sense." Carol looked up again at the sun, standing still and shining bright. "Nothing like that's gonna happen. You're the king! And look at me. We're big!" He held his hands out expansively, broadening his enormous chest. "How can big guys like us worry about a tiny little thing like the sun?"

Max smiled weakly.

"You want me to eat it, King?" Carol said. "I'll jump up and eat that sucker before it can be dead or whatever." He jumped up, grabbing for the sun with his hairy paw.

Max laughed. "No, no. Don't," he said.

"You sure? It looks juicy."

"No, that's okay."

Carol put his hand on Max's head. "Okay. But you let me know. C'mon, we're almost there."

They walked through the lava, and then through a maze of tall, sharp silver stones shaped like teeth. There were thousands of them, all around.

"Just wait till we get there," Carol said, getting excited. "You're gonna love it. If anyone would understand it, it would be you. I see the way you watch things. You have good eyes."

Just then, an enormous animal — at least sixty feet

tall — lumbered slowly by, far off in the distance, over a desert ridge. It looked a lot like a dog.

"What's *that*?" Max asked, expecting to hear about a mythical creature with a mythical name.

Carol squinted and put his hand over his eyes to see better. "Oh, that's a dog," he said. "I don't talk to that guy anymore."

Max and Carol climbed up a steep hillside of oversized silver stones. Carol's huge legs made climbing the giant rocks much easier than for Max. While Carol jumped from one to the next like he was walking up stairs, Max struggled to keep up, having to find toeholds in each boulder.

When he was just about too exhausted to continue, Max heard Carol's voice from high above:

"We're here. Or I am at least."

Max looked up to see Carol standing in the entrance to a magnificent and dizzyingly intricate wooden structure built into the side of the mountain. The design was utterly its own, curvy like the homes they'd demolished on the first night, but it was far more complex and grand, a multi-tiered palace somehow anchored perpendicularly to the side of the cliff. Finally Max reached the flat stone on which Carol stood. Carol was grinning like mad.

"Ready?" Carol asked.

Max was heaving from the climb, but he couldn't wait. He nodded.

Carol looked around to make sure no one had followed them, and then led Max inside.

CHAPTER XXIV

The room was high-ceilinged and wide and full of peach-colored light. It was a studio of some kind, messy and full of projects — kite-like contraptions hanging from above, hexagonal boxes all over the floor, everything carved with dizzying detail, patterns upon patterns. There were a hundred skylights above, all of them oval and allowing the brilliant sun, filtered by some kind of flesh-colored glass, into the room.

Max walked around slowly, taking everything in. There were contraptions everywhere, facsimiles of animals carved or assembled from wood and stone and gems. On the walls were endless drawings, paintings, diagrams, plans.

On the main worktable, an entire city was laid out, almost twenty feet long and six feet tall — buildings shaped like mountains and hills in an organized, almost grid-like format. The city's architecture was similar to that of the village they destroyed — long straight lines, slowly curving, twisting like reluctant corkscrews. The details were immaculate and painstaking. It looked like it would have taken ten years to make. It was a model world — controllable, predictable, tidy.

"Did you make this?" Max asked, his voice an awed whisper.

"Yeah," Carol said, looking at it anew through Max's eyes.

"It's really good," Max said. "I wish I could shrink myself down and get inside it."

Carol's mouth opened wide into a goofy grin. "Well then, you should!" He guided Max under the table, where he had carved open a hole in the platform. Max popped up through the hole and now was in the middle of the model world.

"I've only shown this one other time, and she didn't really get it," Carol said, seeming pained even recalling the memory. Realizing his darkening mood, Carol changed the subject. "Oh! Put your eyes right here."

Carol's huge paws moved Max's head so his eyes were at the street level of the model city. As Max was focused on the minutiae of the buildings, he heard the sound of water. Carol had tilted a jug, and soon water slowly flowed through the streets.

"I always thought it would be better if we had rivers to get around from place to place," Carol said.

Max watched from ground level. The streets were now paved with water, and a tiny boat sailed through an intersection, in and out of view.

Now Max could see that the tiny boat held tiny,

crudely carved facsimiles of Carol and Katherine. The rowboat soon merged with a boulevard carrying many other canoes, all holding creatures. Soon the canoe carrying Carol and Katherine took a turn — at a fork, it sailed left while the rest went right — and in a moment it ran into a pole, knocking the two models out of the boat. They promptly sank.

Max looked up at Carol, astounded. Carol didn't notice — he was carefully working on a new structure for the model city. With great delicacy he carved into a thin sheet of wood with his pinkie claw.

It amazed Max how Carol, roped with muscle and easily seven hundred pounds, could work with such finesse. Max's gaze drifted back to the city. He looked underneath the table. There was nothing there, just a few drips from where the streets leaked.

"What would happen under the city, with all this water?" Max asked.

"I don't know," Carol said, his curiosity piqued.

Max examined the underside more thoroughly.

"You could have a whole underwater world. It would be upside down and everything could hang from the ceiling like stalactites. There'd be fish under the streets. And the subway trains would have to be submarines."

"Wow," Carol said, pondering it all. "That's a good point. Yeah. I like your brain, Max."

Max smiled. It was the first time anyone had ever said that to him. He loved that Carol liked his brain.

Carol looked over the city, seeing it through Max's eyes. "I love making buildings. This is the first one I ever made.

I try to make buildings that feel good to be in. Like this. C'mere."

Max took a step toward him. Carol suddenly enveloped Max in a bear hug.

"What's that feel like?" Carol asked.

"Ummm, hairy? Warm. Good."

"Yeah. I want to build a whole world like that. Have you ever been in a place that should feel good, but it feels out of control, like you're really small? Like where all the people are made out of wind, like you don't know what they're going to do next?"

Max nodded vigorously.

"When?" Carol asked.

"Well," Max said, surprised to be put on the spot. "This one time I went to my friend's house, and everyone in his family had these huge mouths but no ears. And where they were supposed to have ears they just had more mouths so they couldn't listen."

Carol was rapt.

"And when you talked," Max continued, "they couldn't even hear you. Even the mom's boyfriend had three mouths. And all they would do all the time is eat and talk."

Carol shivered theatrically. "Ugh. Who wants to be in a house like that? We need a place where people don't have three mouths, where the sun can't die on you and a mountain can't just fall on you. I want to make a place where only the things you *want to* happen happen."

After a few hours in the studio, Max and Carol felt they should make their way back to the others.

"Your royal subjects await," Carol said.

Max nodded solemnly. "It is so," he said.

But on the way down the rocky hillside, Max had an idea, and it seemed an idea that needed to be enacted for the good of the island.

He wanted Carol to lift one of the enormous rocks on the hillside — one of the steps that led to the studio — and throw it off the cliff and into the ocean below.

Carol smiled. "No, really?" he asked.

"Yes," Max said seriously. "That's an order."

"Good enough for me," Carol said, and squatted before the boulder. With a loud grunt he lifted the rock, his face a mess of contortion and veins. He shuffled a quick few steps over to the edge of the cliff, and then heaved it down. They both watched as it tumbled and ricocheted violently, bouncing off the face of the cliff and disappearing into the sea below. Along the way, it brought about a hundred other rocks with it.

Max turned to Carol, grinning. "Wow, that was a good idea! Let's do more!"

Max pointed to another boulder, and Carol duly lifted it and tossed it down the side of the cliff. Again it brought a good chunk of the cliffside with it.

"All right, who wants it next?" Max asked, looking at the remaining boulders. He looked at three of them, pointing to each one, eyeing each with great suspicion.

He pointed at one: "You?" The boulder said nothing.

"You?" This next boulder, too, chose to remain silent.

The third boulder, Max thought, was giving him a

smartalecky look. "Carol, get 'im," he commanded.

So Carol lifted this boulder and threw it down the cliff. As it bounced toward the sea, a mini-avalanche roared into the ocean and landed with a long loud hiss.

With all the boulders that had previously led to Carol's studio now in the sea below, it would make getting there difficult in the future, but Max and Carol weren't thinking of that right now. Max wasn't, at least. He was thinking of just how much fear they'd struck in the hearts of the rocks on the hillside, and probably all the rocks on the island.

Max laughed till he snorted. "Man oh man, these rocks are really scared of us!"

Carol smiled. "That they are, King. And they should be. Well done."

CHAPTER XXV

When Max and Carol returned to the site of the beasts' former homes, Max could now see the result of the previous night's merrymaking. There was wreckage everywhere. Charred trees and branches. Huge holes in the ground. And every one of their nest-homes was splintered beyond recognition, stamped into the ground.

The other beasts were gathered amid the devastation, some pacing, others with their arms crossed, all of them looking impatient. There was no sign of Katherine.

Ira was chewing on Judith's arm nervously, and when they all caught sight of Max and Carol descending the hillside to join them, Ira removed his teeth from her limb to speak.

"Where were you? We've just been here. Alone."

The others murmured in a snarling sort of way. Max reached under the remains of the fire and retrieved his crown. He put it on, wincing. It was still hot.

"Without our king," Judith added, and slapped Ira's mouth away from her arm. He'd left a row of deep teeth marks.

Now all of the creatures — Judith, Ira, Douglas, the Bull, and Alexander — encircled Max, looking greatly displeased. As they closed in on him, the smell was tremendous. During their rumpusing, the beasts had perspired a large amount, and now they smelled like vinegar and hummus. Max wondered if he should be worried, given that the beasts were closing in on him much the same way they had the previous night. He would have been more worried were Carol not standing behind him. Even so, he knew he needed to explain his absence.

"I had to see my kingdom," Max said, trying to sound as royal as possible. "To survey it. Carol gave me a tour."

The wave of their anger seemed to retreat for a moment, then roared back.

"How come we weren't invited?" Judith asked. "I could have shown you all that. I wouldn't have enjoyed it, but I would have done it. Probably. If I felt inspired."

"Judith, stop," Carol said, putting his hand on her shoulder. "It was my job to give the tour and I gave it."

"I didn't want to go on the tour anyway," Ira said.

"See?" Carol said. "No one missed out on anything. Everything is as it should be."

There was a grudging chorus of acceptance of this explanation. Judith sat down, put her head on her chin, and looked up to Max.

"So Max," started Judith. "Or King. What is it, anyway? King Max or what?"

"It's King, Judith," Carol answered.

She grinned. "Hmm. King Judith, yeah. I like the sound of that." This got a chuckle out of Alexander. "So King Max," Judith continued. "What kind of king are you going to be?"

Carol's face tightened. "Judith, don't— "

"I'm just *asking* him. You got to walk around the island all day, no doubt talking about all of us, who of us was good and who was not as good, and meanwhile we've been here suffering."

Carol rolled his eyes. "Suffering? Really?"

Judith sniffled. "Yeah," she said, quietly. "Suffering with all the questions. And the doubt."

"And the void," Ira added.

"And the void," Judith repeated. "Almost forgot about the void. Ira's feeling the void. You know how Ira feels about the void." Seeing Max's blank look, she explained: "He doesn't like the void. Makes him feel hollow. And when he feels hollow, he chews on me, and that annoys me. And when I'm annoyed, I chew on small things made of bones and blood."

Ira, now chewing on Judith's arm again, whispered loudly in Judith's ear: "And the hammers..."

"Right," Judith said, "remember the hammers, Max? You had this whole story about the hammers, and how there was this king who could make them happy. Well, the hammers are unhappy, Max. What about the hammers? It's been a whole day and so far nothing's changed. The hammers are displeased."

Carol laughed, dismissing her question. "Judith, please.

Tell me you're not happy right now. We're all happy." He turned around, finding a single tree still standing against the stark landscape. "Tree, tell me you're unhappy." The tree did not answer. Now he turned to a group of rocks, one of which Douglas had been wrestling the previous night. "Rocks, tell me if you feel misunderstood." The rocks did not respond. Now with arms outstretched, Carol looked to the sky. "Sky, speak up if you feel unloved." There was no answer. Now he turned back to Judith. "See, everything else in the world is perfectly content."

Max smiled at Carol's theatrics, and Carol smiled back. Carol then took Judith's head into his mouth. Max froze, thinking something violent was about to happen, but instead Carol shook her head affectionately, like a dog playing with a chew toy.

Judith laughed. "Yeah, yeah, okay, I understand, you've got yours, Carol," she said, freeing herself and wiping Carol's saliva from her ears, "but he's everyone's king. What's he going to do for us?"

"Right. Sure," Carol said. "I get it. I know. But just give him a chance. Max has a lot of great ideas. His brain is the best I've ever seen." Now he turned to Max. "Go ahead, Max, tell them your plan to make everything better for everyone always for all time."

CHAPTER XXVI

Again Max reached into the dark velvet of his brain and found something. Was it a gem? He wasn't sure.

"How about a parade?" he said.

He got only blank stares. No one knew what a parade was. But Max loved parades, had been in parades every year since he was born, every year but last year, when he had to be at his dad's apartment, doing nothing all day except missing the parade that he was supposed to be in.

He had been invited to ride on the hood of one of the mini cars, the size of a kayak, driven by the Rotarians. He'd practiced with Mr. Leland, an oval-faced older man who wore a fez not just during parades but at all times. Some people called him Fez, and every time someone called him Fez he pretended to be baffled by the source of the nickname. Then, after a moment of deep thought, he would say, "Oh, because of the hat!" That put the nicknamers in their place every time. Nicknamers are usually the least creative people in the world, he said.

Anyway, the parade landed on one of the days Max was supposed to be with his dad in the city. Since he'd left, his dad had tried to avoid all situations where he would run into one or two or a few hundred of Max's mom's friends, so the parade was out.

"A par... What is one of those?" Ira asked.

"A parade?" Max explained that a parade was, first of all, one of the great inventions of mankind. Second, he said, it was the best way to demonstrate to the citizens of any civilization that there was a new king. It would entail Max leading all of his new subjects through the island, stomping very loudly and while singing many songs, and ideally doing so for the benefit of the thousand lesser-animal inhabitants of the island.

"Wow, that sounds pretty good," Douglas said.

And so they lined up, with Max in the lead, scepter in hand. It was decided that they would parade through the forest, around the gully, across the many-colored meadow — this is where the mini-tornadoes dwelled, Max was told, and he'd see them when he saw them — and then finally finishing at the lagoon, where, Max figured, they would take a swim to wash off the exertion of the parade. His parades at home typically ended at the town pool, and he had come to associate the parade's end with a massive free-for-all in the main pool, diving off the high dive and playing Marco Polo deep into the evening.

"Everyone ready?" he asked.

Carol was directly behind him, followed by Douglas. Judith was next, and then Ira, Alexander, and the Bull.

"Where's Katherine?" Max asked.

"We can't wait for her," Carol said quickly.

"She wouldn't want to do this kind of thing anyway," Douglas noted. "She's not much of a joiner, King."

Everyone nodded in agreement.

"That would diminish her *aura*," Judith said, dressing the word aura in garish sarcasm.

Max didn't like parading without the full retinue, but a parade like this, all ready to go, couldn't wait. Max raised his scepter high, straightened his crown, and took a deep breath.

"Forward march!" he yelled.

Max marched in the most parade-like and martial way he could manage, pumping his knees and thrusting the scepter over his head with every step.

The rest of the paraders followed suit, and, at Max's urging, improvised however they saw fit. Carol began marching with both of his arms over his head like a ghoul. Douglas marched with his feet shuffling side-to-side, which seemed much more difficult and tiring than necessary, but Max thought it gave the parade a certain panache. Judith and Ira were marching in a more or less traditional way, forward and high-stepping, though Ira, with his poor balance, was having trouble maintaining a straight line. Max couldn't see the Bull or Alexander very well, but he trusted that they knew what they were doing and were making the parade proud.

After parading for about an hour, through sparse forest,

much of it charred and crushed by the rumpus the previous night, Max was beginning to lament the one conspicuously missing part of the parade: spectators.

Just when he was wondering what could be done about the problem, he caught sight of what appeared to be hundreds of the sort of tiny cat he'd seen on his way through the woods the previous night. Now they were emerging everywhere along the path, sitting and standing atop the fallen trees. All were watching the parade, as if it were the first such demonstration they had ever seen. And, Max thought, it probably was.

When the other paraders noticed the cats watching, they paraded with extra effort, stomping higher and shuffling more intensely. And the extra effort seemed to attract more watchers. There were suddenly thousands of eyes along the route, most of them attached to the cats but also to thin tendrils of what looked like ferns. Max looked closer, guessing them to be some kind of land-dwelling anemones, with hundreds of eyes, each sitting atop a long twisting stalk. Max couldn't tell if they were able to think, let alone understand the greatness of the parade, but it hardly mattered. As Max paraded forward, all he could see were the eyeballs, all unblinking, all rapt.

They were about halfway to the lagoon, according to Douglas's estimate, and Max was beginning to tire. He had an idea which seemed to solve his tiredness problem while also remaining true to the parameters of parades.

He climbed up Douglas's leg and shoulders and rode for a time there, his scepter pointing the way. But after a few minutes there, Max was getting bored, so he decided to jump, like a spider monkey, from one set of shoulders to the next. It was far trickier than spider monkeys made it look, but every time Max would slip, an enormous paw would be there to restore him to his perch. Max was confident he would get better at the jumping in the future, but in any case it would be how he would travel from now on. It was quicker than walking, and he liked the view from up above far more.

As he sat on the Bull's head, and while the rest of the paraders paraded, his mind spun through the possibilities — all the things he could and should do with seven giant playmates — and the first and most obvious one seemed to be that he and they needed to make a ship of some kind. He jumped over to Ira and began, mid-thought:

"Yeah, it's gonna be a vampire ship," Max said, "the biggest and fastest vampire ghost ship ever created. And we're gonna need lots of trees. We're gonna need um... twenty... No, more! We're gonna need a hundred of the biggest tree trunks on the island. Ira, you get the trees."

"Okay," Ira said.

"And lots of rope. And some sails." He jumped onto Douglas. "Douglas, you have to get the sails. The finest sails known to man!"

"Yes, King Max," Douglas replied, and with his claw made some kind of notation on his arm.

"I'll be the captain, and Judith, you'll be in charge of speed. You have to make sure we have good wind." Judith seemed very pleased to have been asked. "And Ira, you can steer the boat. What's the person called who steers the boat?"

"The captain?" Ira offered uncertainly.

"Okay, well, I'll steer the ship. *I'm* the captain."

"And I'm in charge of wind?" Judith said. Her eyes seemed to be envisioning this new and vital role.

Max nodded. "Wind and weather, yeah. And speed."

"What about me?" Alexander asked.

"You can be the lookout," Max said.

"No, I don't want to look out," Alexander said. "Or maybe I would if the ship was different and I was the captain instead of you."

Max didn't know how to answer Alexander. He made a note to try to avoid him altogether in the future.

"Psst. Hey King!"

Max turned to see Katherine hiding in the hollow of an enormous tree. She beckoned him over. Relieved to be away from the goat, Max jumped off Douglas's shoulders and over to her.

"I need to talk to you," she said.

"Really?" Max said. "About what?" He didn't want to leave the parade, so he tried to lure her into talking while walking with the group.

But she didn't want that.

"We need a little privacy," she said, pulling him from the path.

Max really didn't think he should be leaving his own parade, but there was something so intriguing about Katherine. They wouldn't miss him for a little bit.

"Grab here," Katherine said, indicating the fur on the back of her neck. "Hold tight."

CHAPTER XXVII

Max did, and immediately his feet left the earth. With Max on her back, and with incredible speed, Katherine climbed the tree she'd been hiding in. She climbed so fast, chipmunk-style, that he could barely hold on. In seconds they were at the top of a fifty-foot tree, its leaves a pale purple, and Katherine was resting on a platform she had arranged between the tree's two highest boughs. She placed Max on his feet, and he found himself standing atop a ten-foot square wooden perch.

"You like it up here?" she asked.

He nodded, awed. From the platform he could see the whole island — the cauliflower forests, the burnt-red desert, the black and blue ravines, the ever-grinning ocean. He looked down, where Katherine was laying on her stomach on the narrow platform.

"Oh man, that climb got me sore. Can you walk on my back?" she asked.

Max didn't know what she was talking about.

She looked up to him and rolled her eyes. "It's sore. You think you could walk on it?"

Max had never been asked to walk on someone's back before.

"What, like actually step on you?" he said.

"Yup, step on me, and then walk around."

Max couldn't wrap his head around this.

"C'mon, just step on," she said.

He aimed his foot toward her torso.

"King, do it!" she said, grabbing his foot.

He gingerly began to walk on top of her. She was soft in some places and in others he could feel the ropes of muscle underneath the heavy fur.

"Oh, that feels good," she said.

Max was trying not to hurt her, while also trying hard to keep his balance. Any slip and he would fall off Katherine, off the platform, and down fifty feet. Katherine didn't seem to be concerned at all about the danger.

"Now jump up and down really quick, like you're walking on fire," she said.

He did so as best he could.

"Good, good," she said. "That's the only way to get rid of the knots."

Max slowed his jumping, hoping that he could be finished as soon as possible. "Done?" he asked.

"Sure. Thanks, King," she said, and quickly rolled onto her back, forcing Max to step quickly, log-rolling-style, until he was standing on her stomach.

"Please go slower," he asked.

Katherine looked up at him, as if assessing whether she should ask him what she wanted to ask him.

"Hey Max, you ever feel like you're, like, stuck under other people?" she said, squinting up at him, seeming immensely relieved to have said it. "Sometimes I feel like I'm trapped under people... like in a bad way. You know what I mean?"

Max began to formulate an answer but she didn't seem to need one.

"I don't know," she continued, "I feel like I'm constantly burdened by everyone's *issues*. You know?"

Max thought he knew. Or did he? He wasn't sure, but it didn't matter. He just liked being with her, alone with her. She seemed interested in him, in being only with him and talking only to him, and he was having trouble breathing.

She smiled at him. "I was about to go crazy before you showed up. You're different, you know? You're..." She seemed on the verge of saying something very serious but then retreated. "You know, you've got less hair, you're cleaner... You smell better. You don't smell great, but better."

Max laughed.

"King?" It was a distant voice, maybe Carol's, from far below. "Max?"

Max jumped off Katherine's stomach and tried to peer through the treetops to find the parade. He knew he needed to get back.

Katherine sighed. "Yeah, I know. You're the *king* and all. I'm sorry for taking you away from your kingly subjects. Hold on. I know a shortcut."

Max again held onto the scruff of her neck and immediately Katherine leapt from her platform — thirty feet up, a hundred feet forward, and then descended into what seemed like a mess of trees twenty feet down. But as they fell closer, another platform became visible, and Max realized they would be landing on it. He braced himself for painful impact but at the moment they touched the platform, they were high in the air again. Katherine had managed to touch the platform's surface the tiniest fragment of a second before bounding off again, onto the next tree and the next platform. She leapt and bounded this way, more agile than any kangaroo or frog, for six more trees, each journey more thrilling than any roller coaster or bungee jump Max had ever known or seen and the only problem was the barf on his wolf suit. He threw up twice, yes, but it was a good kind of throwing up.

Finally Max felt them descending farther, down, down. He could see the lagoon ahead, a green body of water in the shape of a sleeping dog, and just before the lagoon he could see the group of beasts making their way there.

CHAPTER XXVIII

They came to earth slowly, as if tied to a hundred parachutes. They had beaten the group to the lagoon and Katherine made sure everyone had taken note of their entrance. No one was impressed, and Carol did not seem pleased at all. His face was twisted into a scowl.

Max ran over to him.

"Hey! You ready to swim?" he asked.

Carol shrugged.

"What's the matter?" Max asked.

"Where were you guys?" Carol asked.

"Who? Me and Katherine? We just took a different route."

"But you were supposed to lead the parade."

"I did."

"And then you didn't."

There was a new sharpness to Carol's tone that Max couldn't figure out. Was he really mad about something?

"Well, that's when I had to see something with Katherine. Now let's swim. Do you like the water?"

"No," Carol said flatly. "And I don't like sailing, either. Remember?"

Max didn't remember.

"I heard you were talking about building a ship with everyone else. Why would you do that?"

"How do you mean?"

"Why would you need a ship, Max? You're thinking of leaving already?"

"No, no," Max said. "This would just be for fun. Or emergencies." Carol's face had darkened and his eyes had gone small. His expression scattered Max's brain so much he started babbling: "It'll have a trampoline. And a big aquarium. An aquarium under the water, inside the ship, where we keep the fish and squids and stuff we like…"

The explanation was doing no good.

"But I thought we said we were bored by sailing," Carol said. "Isn't that what you said just this morning? We talked about killing anything boring but now you want to *sail*? The most boring thing of all?"

"Well," Max mumbled, but he hadn't a clue how to reconcile the two states of mind. "We don't have to build it. It was just an idea."

"And why would you build it without me? I'm the one here who knows how to build things."

"I *wasn't* going to build it without you," Max said. "I was just telling everyone about it. We were all going to build it together. Everyone was."

"But it doesn't seem like you want to be together.

Otherwise you wouldn't have gone your different route with Katherine. What's so great about her route anyway?"

Max had to think. This was getting too complicated too quickly. He felt his brain splitting and hiding. If only he could get Carol into the water and playing Marco Polo, he wouldn't be upset about these little things.

"Let's just swim," Max said. "Please?"

"You guys go ahead," Carol said, and then went off to a dark corner of the lagoon to stew. Max watched him sit down, throw his chin into his hands, and glower. He was tempted to go and talk to him, but he knew that time would heal this wound, which he assumed was small, superficial even. He hoped that Carol's fiery mood would be cooled by the sight of merriment all around him.

"C'mon everyone, let's swim!" Max said.

He ran from the grass, up a small embankment, and did a cannonball into the water.

No one followed.

"Okay everyone, do what I did," he yelled. "Who can do the best cannonball? Katherine?"

She shook her head. "I don't really do stuff like that," she said. "I'm fine here."

"Douglas?" Max said.

Douglas seemed flattered to have been singled out, and so got ready to follow Max into the water.

"Hold on!" Carol said.

Douglas stopped. Max turned. Carol was on his knees at the edge of the lagoon, his ear to the mossy ground. "What is it?" Max said.

Carol held his hand up in a wait-a-second gesture. He

closed his eyes, listening intently to the earth for what seemed like a full minute, and then got up. "It's probably nothing," he said, knowing he had everyone's rapt attention.

"What was it?" Max asked.

Carol didn't answer.

"You don't think it's anything?" Ira asked.

The other beasts were frozen, their eyes huge with concern. Carol stood for a moment, a look of great thoughtfulness on his face.

"It's nothing, don't worry about it," Carol said, in a way clearly meant to cause more concern. "Have fun. I'll tell you if we need to worry."

Max wasn't ready to give up on the lagoon, on Marco Polo and the prospect of finishing the parade the way it needed to be finished.

"Okay, get in now!" Max yelled. He began splashing Douglas and Ira, but now no one wanted to go in the water. They were still watching Carol, who periodically got on his knees to listen to the ground.

"I order you to swim!" Max said.

No one moved.

Finally Max had to get out and do the job himself. He grabbed each potential swimmer by the hand, dragged them to the water, and pushed them in. He was pleasantly surprised by how well they all floated — they were like buoys, resting atop the surface with incredible ease.

Soon he had them all in the water, and was trying to get them to listen to the rules of Marco Polo. "Okay, so you have to close your eyes. Wait, I close my eyes. Then

I swim around after you say Marco. No, I say Marco, and then you say Polo. And when you say Polo I try to catch whoever said it. Or I can hear you when you say that, so I go toward the sound— "

The mention of sound only got the creatures thinking again about whatever Carol was hearing in the ground, so they focused their attention on him. And he seemed to take the task very seriously. His mouth was moving silently, as if he were repeating whatever horrible things the ground was telling him.

Max, though, was determined to make the lagoon a success. If he could only get everyone in the water, he knew that they would love Marco Polo, and would forget the chatter and whatever else was on their minds.

"Hey Carol," Max said, "you think it'd be good if someone went down the waterfall?"

Carol shrugged.

"Ira, go down the waterfall," Max ordered.

Ira sat for a moment, then, resigned, stood and slowly climbed up the cliff wall. At the top, where the water looked downward and fell, he sat down, and with absolutely no joy or inspiration at all, he allowed himself to be taken over. But he wasn't positioned correctly. He descended in a morose kind of belly-flop form, and Max knew that he would land with a huge and painful slap.

And so he did. The sound, like a wet shirt thrown against cement, was almost as painful to the ears as it no doubt felt to Ira.

It seemed like minutes before he emerged from the water, shuddering. He floated on his back for some time, moaning, weeping, sniffling and then moaning some more. The beasts all gave Max terrible looks.

The lagoon was not a success, and Max was quickly running out of ideas to create any kind of diversion or happiness in the lives of his subjects.

"Psst." Max looked up to find Katherine up above him. She was hanging from a low bough of a tree. "Let's get out of here," she said.

Max was so happy to see her, and was so ready to leave with her, to be free, even momentarily, of the obligations of pleasing everyone. He lifted his arms to allow her to raise him to the trees when—

"Wait!" Carol said, dropping to his knees. "Listen!" He rested his ear against the earth.

Everyone went quiet and rigid.

The look on Carol's face grew grave.

"What? What is it?" Judith asked.

"It doesn't sound good," Carol answered.

The others scampered around Carol, with Douglas and Judith almost trampling Max to get there.

"What is it? Vibrations?" Douglas asked.

"Whispering?" Judith added. "Chatter?"

Carol lowered his head and nodded. "Vibrations, chatter, *and* whispering, I'm afraid," he said.

"Oh no," Ira moaned. "Not again."

"Does it sound close?" Alexander whined.

Carol gave them an expression that seemed to say, "I don't know for sure, but it very well might be right underneath us, ready to devour all of us at once."

"Then what are we still doing here?" Judith wailed.

"Run!" Douglas yelled.
And so they ran.

CHAPTER XXIX

The beasts took off in seven different directions. Then, one by one, they turned to see where Carol was running, and they changed directions to follow him. Even Katherine dropped from the branches above to run and to follow Carol. Max did too.

"Carol!" he yelled. Max was running faster than he'd ever run and could barely speak, but he needed to know what was happening. "Why are we running?" he managed to say, heaving and holding his side.

Carol didn't answer him. He didn't even look his way.

"Carol!" he yelled. Carol was going thirty miles an hour, Max figured. Max couldn't hope to keep up. Just as Carol disappeared down a ravine, Max spotted Ira following him.

"Ira!" Max yelled. Ira was slower, but still far faster than he looked. Heaving and crying, he almost ran over Max, seeming not to have seen him at all. He didn't say a word as he sped by.

Not one of the beasts seemed concerned about leaving their king behind. They were barreling into anything, knocking any and all in-the-way foliage flat. They were huffing and moaning, their eyes tearing and their arms grabbing at the air in front of them. They were crazed. All Max could do was follow the wide swath their stampede cut through the trees and underbrush.

Max ran until he was ready to throw up. Leaning against a tree and catching his breath, he finally spotted them beyond the woods, all six beasts, in a many-colored meadow. The grass there was long, soft, and arrayed in a patchwork of clashing colors — ochre and black and violet and fuchsia. The beasts were all gathered in the middle, in a loose circle, heaving. A few had collapsed on the ground. As Max approached, they seemed to take little or no notice of him.

Max found Carol. "What was it?"

"What was what?" Carol asked.

"The sound. Whatever we were running from."

"You don't know?" Carol asked.

Max shook his head.

Carol looked surprised, or feigned surprise.

"You really don't know?" he asked again.

Suddenly Carol was spun around. It was Judith, her claw on Carol's shoulder.

"Where's Douglas?" she asked, a panicked look on her face.

Carol shrugged. He turned to Max. "You see Douglas out there?"

Max hadn't. Carol gave him an exasperated look, as if

to say *What* do *you know, King?*

"Maybe he wasn't with us in the first place," Carol said.

"Of course he was," Katherine said.

But everyone else seemed suddenly unsure.

Katherine turned to Max. "Did *you* see Douglas with us?"

Max had, and was about to say so, but Carol interrupted him, placing his gigantic paw over Max's mouth. "Don't do that, Katherine. Don't bring him into it. Douglas did not come."

"Of course he did," she said, astonished. "He was with us a few minutes ago."

"Sorry. You're wrong," Carol said dismissively.

"I can't believe you," Katherine said. "Do you really not notice who's around you? Are you really that self-centered that you can't remember which four or five of us are near at any given time? Do you look at or hear any of us?"

This made Carol boil. But before he could formulate an answer, Katherine turned to the rest of the group.

"Okay, whoever thinks he *was* with us, stand up. And whoever thinks he wasn't, sit down."

Everyone began to sit down and stand accordingly, though they all were apprehensive to be picking sides.

Carol was exasperated. "No, no! Whoever thinks he *wasn't* with us, stand up. And whoever thinks he *was*, lie down."

"No," Katherine said, her face reddening, "*I* was already standing! Why do you have to do that, even change the way I set it up? You make everything ten times harder than it needs to be."

"No I don't."

"Yes you do."

"Do not."

Katherine turned back to the group, who were all watching the debate intently, like children at a puppet show. "Okay, everyone who thinks Carol makes things ten times harder than they need to be, raise your left hand. If you think he *doesn't* make things harder, raise your *right* hand."

Everyone began, tentatively, to raise one arm or the other.

"Wait," Judith said. "Should we be sitting down, too? Or is that part over? I don't like sitting down when people tell me to sit down. It takes the pleasure out of it—"

"Forget it," Katherine said. "It's not worth it." And she walked away, disappearing into the forest shadows before leaping upward.

A moment later, a rustling came from the woods, and Douglas emerged from between two trees and entered the clearing. He looked dazed, exhausted.

"Did you find out what it was?" Judith asked him.

Douglas shook his head. "No."

"Did you hear anything?" Ira asked.

"No. Or maybe," he said. "I don't know. I did hear a loud, rhythmic sound, like a huffing. It was really loud, and lasted the whole time I was running. Now it's gone though."

Ira and Alexander looked worried. Carol nodded solemnly, as if this, unfortunately, confirmed his suspicions. Only Judith thought to second-guess it. She rolled her eyes and sighed elaborately.

"That was your own *breathing*, Douglas. Of course it

stopped. You stopped *running*." But though Judith was skeptical of Douglas's account of the sounds underground, she didn't doubt the existence of the chatter. "Carol," she said, "when you heard it, did it ever sound like huffing?"

Carol was diplomatic. "I think it might have, somewhere down there. And it sounds different to different ears, of course. You might hear something more jagged and angry, Judith. It might be chatter specifically about you, and all the things you've done wrong. Ira might hear something open and hollow, like an empty, void-ish sound, the sound of a well with no bottom. They really know how to get to us."

Judith was staring hard at Max. "So what should we do, King?"

"About what?" he asked.

"What do you mean, about what? About the sounds that run under the ground and are mean to us. What else?" she said. "We need to kill it dead, right, Carol?"

Carol nodded.

Max had no plan at all. "So what does it sound like again?" he asked.

Judith was apoplectic. "Wait. You don't know about the chatter? I don't know what's worse — the chatter, or the fact that our king doesn't know anything about it. How can you rule this place if you don't know about the sounds in the ground?"

"I didn't say I didn't know," he said. "I just was asking you guys what *you* thought it was. Where I come from the chatter just sounds different."

Max got on his knees and listened to the earth. "Yeah, I hear it for sure. But it's just quieter than where I come from. Our chatter is super-loud and it sounds like teeth."

This had everyone's attention.

"So what did you do about it?" Douglas asked.

"Oh, a lot of things," Max said, having no idea at all.

"Like what?" Ira asked.

"Well, one thing is that we yelled a lot. We yelled out in the air a lot because then we didn't hear the chatter."

This didn't seem to impress anyone.

"And the other thing was that we stomped on the ground really hard. We stomped like we did at the parade. We did that all the time, to let the sounds know how big we were. Sometimes with heavy boots."

This was somewhat more convincing to the beasts.

"Okay," Judith said. "So you scared it with the boots. What else? I'm assuming you got rid of it?"

"Oh yeah, pretty quickly. It was easy," Max said.

"How?" Carol asked, his eyes pleading.

Now Max was up a creek. He couldn't see or hear the thing they feared, but he had to think of a way to kill it. He was sure he could find a way to kill anything in the world if he could *see* it — especially with seven giants on his side — but if he knew nothing about it? He was stuck. He had to stall for time.

"I can't tell you today..." he said, "but tomorrow I can. Tomorrow I will." It was lame, Max knew it was lame, but it was working. They were nodding, as if acknowledging that such a problem needed a day of kingly consideration. He added the finishing touches to the lie. "I just need to stay here awhile, testing the ground and, uh, seeing which one of my killing methods will work best."

They all nodded vigorously, picturing the many killing methods they knew themselves.

"You heard the king," Carol said, shooing everyone away. "He needs time to think. Let's give him some room." He hustled them out of the meadow. Before he left Max by himself, Carol turned back to him.

"I really hope you kill it, Max," he said. "It would really help us a lot. I feel like I haven't slept in years."

And with that, he left.

CHAPTER XXX

Max took off his heavy crown and sat in the many-colored meadow, alone, trying to piece together exactly how he came to be sitting in the many-colored meadow, alone.

There had been the parade, and that was good. Then the different route with Katherine, which was also very good. But when he arrived at the lagoon, Carol had not been happy about him leaving the parade. Carol seemed upset about Max's time alone with Katherine. Max had to be careful about that in the future. He also needed to be careful about Ira and water — Ira definitely didn't seem to like bellyflopping down a waterfall. And Judith didn't like sitting down on command; she liked to sit when and how she wanted to sit. That seemed easy to remember.

All Max had to do, then, was to make sure that he didn't upset Carol by spending time alone with Katherine, or upset Katherine by being alone with Carol, and he had to make sure Judith was being entertained and that

Ira was being kept from the void. He wasn't sure what the Bull wanted, but he knew for his own safety he needed to steer clear of Alexander, who'd had a very personal problem with Max from the start. Was that everything he needed to think about?

Oh, food. There was food to think about. Could it be that he hadn't eaten since he'd left home? He really hadn't. Nothing the beasts had eaten so far was edible for Max, and on his own he had no idea where to get food, or how to recognize it. And he couldn't go into the woods looking for it, because it was getting dark quickly, and he'd seen snakes in the trees, and spiders the size of his fist, and knew there were countless other dangers unseen.

He felt reasonably safe in the middle of the meadow, though, and he realized that to remain safe all he needed to do was stay awake until the dawn. Easy. And while waiting for the sun, he only needed to solve the problem of the sounds in the ground that Carol heard whenever he was worried about something else.

Not expecting to hear anything, Max put his ear to the grass. Indeed, he heard nothing. There was no sound at all. But Carol knew this island far better than he did, and Carol's ears might be better than his — and anyway, whether Max heard the sound or not, he needed to find it and kill it, or at least get the beasts to stop thinking about it.

He had faced similar challenges at home, with his mom, a dozen times. She would come home drained, collapsing on the couch or sometimes even the floor, and Max would find a way to entertain her or soothe her or somehow bring her to a different, happier, place. Sometimes he brought her a piece or two of his Halloween candy. Sometimes he would put the candy in the music box on the mantel. He'd get it down and turn the crank and present it to her, so when she opened the top the music started and the candy was there, always something she liked, like Bit o' Honey. Sometimes he drew her something — a dragon getting its head cut off by a knight or a whale with arms and a mustache. There were a bunch of ways, he was sure, to lead someone out of a dark corridor of the mind.

Just then a sound came from the encircling woods. It was a high-pitched sound, something like a hyena's laugh crossed with a woodpecker's knocking. It was terrifying and arrhythmic, and growing louder. At any moment Max expected some animal to burst from the woods and beeline toward him.

He knew he wouldn't sleep this night. He would wait until first light and then go looking for Carol or Katherine, or anyone, really. And then he would have to set down some rules about leaving him, the king, alone in the middle of a meadow all night. He had to do so without implying that he was afraid of the dark, which he wasn't, but that instead it was for their own good. They needed to be together, all of them, for together they were safer and happier. Or he hoped they would be.

He sat up in the meadow, scanning the forest for movement. Just then another sound came from the opposite woods. This one was a rough, zig-zagging call, trilling upward before ending with a loud sigh, like a truck at rest. It was just as threatening and eerie as the other sound, and soon the first sound and the second were trading calls, as

if in a heated conversation full of threats and recrimina-
tions. Max had to spin back and forth, following the
sounds, looking for anything moving. The fighting, if
that's what it was, seemed to be happening far away and
didn't involve him, but then again, how could he be sure?
He might be the cause of it and very well might be its vic-
tim. And so he had to stay alert.

It was exhausting, but he knew the argument going on
was useful in that it would certainly keep him awake — he
couldn't possibly think of resting while it was all going
on. And that's how he got the idea that he got. He smiled
to himself, laughing even, knowing he'd come up with the
best solution possible to the problem of the underground
whispering plaguing the consciences of the beasts. He
couldn't wait till morning to announce the plan and put it
into action. It was so good he found himself cackling all
night, in sudden and helpless bursts. It was the best plan,
the only plan.

CHAPTER XXXI

Max woke up before dawn, cold and wet with dew. He had somehow fallen asleep, and now he was hungry and thirsty and, he realized with a shudder, he hadn't moved his bowels since he'd left home. His fur smelled terrible and now had a green tint to it — the lagoon water had been full of algae and had gifted Max its thick stench.

And there was no sign of anyone.

But he knew, at least, that he would make everyone happy this day. He had a plan and only had to find the beasts to enact it.

In the pre-dawn light Max could see the tracks they'd made, and could clearly make out Carol's huge foot-prints, leading out of the meadow and toward the cliff. He followed them across the meadow, through a narrow stand of trees, and into a clearing covered with a strange moss, black and yellow, alternating like a checkerboard. Beyond it, the ocean was a frenzy of white. Max scanned the electric blue horizon until he saw what seemed to be a figure sitting on the edge of the cliff, the same cliff where they had howled together on Max's first night.

He ran toward the figure, and when he got close he knew it was Carol, sitting forward, seeming tense.

"Carol!" Max yelled as he approached.

Without turning around, Carol raised his hand, demanding silence. Max stopped about twenty feet away, not knowing what to do next.

Carol remained staring out at the ocean, as if looking for a sign in the ripening sky. As it grew lighter, a crescent-shaped band of orange appeared above the line of the sea. Carol leaned forward, getting dangerously close to the very edge of the cliff.

And then, finally, when the liquid yellow of the sun at last broke through, Carol's body relaxed, and then shook in waves, as if he were laughing or crying. Max couldn't tell. But the spell, whatever it had been, was broken.

Carol turned around.

"Hey Max! You were wrong about the sun dying. Look, it's right here."

Max didn't know how to explain.

"Don't scare me like that again, okay buddy?" Carol said. He spoke cheerfully, as if the distant, rigid Carol of moments before had been illusory, that here was the real Carol, the one who loved Max's brain and who knew how things were supposed to feel, who wanted only the right things to happen.

"How are you, King Max?" Carol asked, putting his hand on Max's shoulder. "What happened to your fur? It's kind of green."

"Algae maybe? I don't know," Max said distractedly. He couldn't worry about his fur at that moment. He wanted to know where all the others were.

"Well, Douglas is over there," Carol said, pointing to a lump in the near distance. Max had walked right past him, thinking his body was an outcropping. "But I don't know where anyone else is. Why do you want to know?"

"I have a plan," Max said.

CHAPTER XXXII

Everyone was gathered around Max. Carol had woken up Douglas and Douglas had raised back his head and had made a bizarre and screeching sound of summoning. The beasts had arrived within minutes from all corners of the island. Everyone, that is, but Katherine. Max decided to proceed without her.

"Okay," he said, "I have the perfect plan. What does everyone here want?" he asked, though the question, for him, was rhetorical.

"We don't have homes," Douglas said. "We've been sleeping outside because you wrecked them."

Max was about to quibble with this claim, but he didn't. He knew his plan would eclipse small concerns like Douglas's. "Okay, fine," he said.

"Some of us are hungry," Alexander said.

"Okay, sure," Max said. "What else? What do you *want*?"

"We want what we want. We want all the things we want," Judith said, matter-of-factly. She brushed Ira's mouth off her shoulder. He'd been chewing again, more than ever, it seemed. There were patches, purple and blue, all over her now, where the fur had been gnawed off.

Ira whispered something in her ear. She nodded. "Oh, and we want no more want."

Max grinned. He really felt like he had the perfect idea to not only address all these concerns, but also those he had recognized himself — the need for togetherness, for camaraderie and entertainment and a sense of purpose. He had expected everyone's first need to be fun, and guessed that they had simply forgotten that this was the first and foremost need of all. When he mentioned it, they would all smack their foreheads in an expression of *Aha*!

"What about fun?" he asked.

They all looked confused.

"Fun, like that lagoon business?" Judith asked. "If that was fun, I'd rather have someone eat my head."

"No, no," Max protested. "I mean *real* fun."

"Oh. *Real* fun," she said, nodding. "Wait. What's that?"

"It's like fun," Max said, "but much better."

They all thought about this, wondering if fun would be the solution. No one spoke up. Each was waiting for someone else to ask the obvious questions. There was a long silence, finally broken when Ira cleared his throat and spoke softly to his toes.

"I'm confused about fun," he said.

Judith exhaled loudly. "Thank god *someone* said it. I was thinking the same thing. What does *want* have to do with *fun*, and what does all of this have to do with the void? Right, Ira?"

Ira shrugged. He was more confused than ever.

Carol shushed them both. "Fun sounds fine. We just need some clarification. Tell us what to do, Max."

Now Max warmed up. He had come up with the whole plan in the many-colored meadow, and now he got to do something he was good at: explaining the game and outlining the rules. He was so convinced that his idea would bring everyone together and put them all in a near-permanent state of bliss that he was hesitant to just blurt it out. He decided to heighten the drama.

"You ready to hear the plan?"

They all nodded, hushed in silence.

"You sure?"

They nodded again. They were sure.

"We're gonna have..." he said, his eyebrows rising and falling conspiratorially, "a war."

"A war? Like a fight?" Ira asked.

Max nodded. "Yeah, we'll pick sides and then battle."

Douglas tilted his head and squinted. "And then everyone will feel better?" he asked, as if just confirming the obvious logic at work.

"Yeah," Max said. "Pretty much."

"And we won't be hungry?" Alexander asked.

Max didn't know, exactly, if a war would make Alexander less hungry. But then again, he thought, if Alexander was having great fun in the middle of a war, how could he possibly be thinking of food? "You won't be hungry at all," Max said confidently.

"And the void?" Ira asked.

"This is the opposite of a void," Max said, though he still didn't know what Ira meant by void. But if a void was an absence of something — or everything — then Max could assure him that the battle was anything but that. A void was small, and a war was big. A void was silence, and a war was loud, all-encompassing, full of astounding things to see and think about. If they were at war, how could they think about the void? Impossible.

Now Judith and Ira and Douglas and Alexander were all very interested. They thought a war sounded like a very good idea. Behind them, the Bull was glaring at Max in the most intense way. If Max could read his expression, he would have to think that of all the beasts, the Bull was least in favor of the plan. But because he didn't talk — he hadn't said anything since Max had gotten to the island — the Bull didn't really have a vote in the matter.

"Okay," Max said. "Who wants to be the Bad Guys?"

No one raised their hand.

Max pointed to Judith. "You can be a Bad Guy." Now he pointed to Alexander. "And you. You're a Bad Guy." Alexander's shoulders slumped. Max almost laughed. How could Alexander have expected to be a Good Guy? Ridiculous. "And now…" Max said, thinking he was being very gracious, "you guys can pick another."

"Okay," Judith said. "We pick you."

Max was taken aback, but only momentarily. It was so loony that he laughed.

"No, I'm a *Good* Guy. I'm the king. I can't be a Bad Guy. I'll pick." He pointed to Ira. "You're a Bad Guy too.

And you… um… And you should have one more…"

Max looked up at the Bull, who looked down menacingly at Max. Max looked to the Bad Guys and indicated the Bull with his thumb. "And he's on… he's with you."

Just then, Katherine emerged from the forest.

Judith scoffed. "Look who's arrived with her aura of mystery and aloofity! She's come to honor us with her presence."

"Don't worry, Judith," Katherine said, not breaking stride. "No one's honoring you."

"Katherine, you're on our team," Max said.

Katherine smiled. She walked over to Max as if she would never have guessed at any other arrangement.

"I got you this," Katherine said, presenting Max with a tangled mess of seaweed. "A gift from me and the sea."

"Uh, okay, thanks…" he said.

"What are we having teams for?" she asked.

"A war," Max said, grinning. "It's gonna be amazing. We're the Good Guys."

"Who else is on our team?" she asked.

Max explained that it was the two of them, and Carol and Douglas. With this, Katherine's smile evaporated.

"Oh," she mumbled.

By now, Carol, Katherine, Douglas, and Max were standing on one side, Judith, Alexander, Ira, and the Bull on the other. Max got ready to explain the rules. He was in his element, inspired by the upcoming battle. "Okay. Now here's the ammunition," he said, picking up a dirt clod. "We're trying to kill the Bad Guys, and what you have to do is find the biggest pieces, the ones that'll stay toge— "

And with a loud thwack, his vision went grey. He'd been hit in the head with a dirt clod as big as a pumpkin. He turned to see that Alexander — he who threw it — was getting another clod ready.

"Was that too soon?" Alexander asked. "Not the kind of war you had in mind?"

CHAPTER XXXIII

Max was briefly stunned by the blindside, but steadied himself. "Run!" he yelled, darting across the clearing and toward the woods, his team in tow. They were chased by a relentless volley of dirt and rocks thrown by the Bad Guys. The element of surprise, which Max thought he knew something about, had given his opponents a great advantage.

Max dove behind a giant tree, which stood in front of a dry and narrow riverbed. It was a perfect bunker from which to plan and execute a counterattack.

Douglas arrived first, jumping into the bunker head-first and coming up smiling. He had been hit repeatedly on the way, but he was okay. Next was Katherine, panting and wiping dirt from her hair and face. Finally Carol slid into the bunker, grinning and sweating. Now all four of them were in the ditch together, breathing heavily and feeling very alive, with a very clear sense of purpose to their lives — live and throw dirt clods or get hit by dirt clods and die. Explosions continued everywhere above them but Max's head was spinning with the incomparable thrill of battle. There really was nothing, he thought, as good as a war.

Max was trying to decide what their next course of action should be when a huge projectile hit the tree trunk behind them and fell to the ground. When it landed, it uncoiled itself and sat up. It wasn't dirt. It was a raccoon. Or a toothy pink animal, striped like a raccoon.

"Hey Larry," Carol said to the animal, stroking its fur. "Sorry about that."

The animal shook its head, dazed. Apparently someone on the Bad Guys' side had balled up this animal, named Larry, and had thrown him at Max's team. Max couldn't decide whether he should ban the use of animal-projectiles or not. But before he could make a decision, and as Larry began to scurry off dizzily, Carol grabbed him, balled him up again, and hurled him back.

There was a shriek from the Bad Guys' camp.

"Larry, you traitor!" Judith yelled.

Max knew that now, while the enemy was distracted, was the time to move out for a counterattack.

"Let's go!" he ordered, and his team followed him out of the bunker. But the second they exposed themselves, they were hit by a barrage of rocks, dirt, and, most disturbingly, a few dozen other animals — tiny cats, snakes, and a sheep-like animal with a head on either end of its body.

"Retreat!" Max yelled, and they slipped back into their

192

bunker. Above and around them, more animals flew. Hundreds of tiny cats, flightless birds, and, with an enormous thump in the trees behind their bunker, something the size and shape of a buffalo, though hairless and yellow. All of the projectile-animals survived the trip, and, after some time recovering, wandered off.

Still, Max decided that something had to be said about this practice of throwing animals. He knew he would have to signal a temporary truce, and for that he would need a white flag. But the only white material he had would be his undershirt or underwear, and could he really take off either to use as a flag? Just then, a volley of tiny cats, a hundred or more this time, all wailing as one, sailed over their bunker, landing in the trees above. They all slipped down the trunks and dropped to the ground, disoriented and not seeming to be having much fun.

Max didn't really see why the animals had to be involved in a war between consenting parties, so he knew he had to do something. He just needed to establish some parameters with the enemy. So without taking off his wolf-suit — he knew not to do that — he maneuvered himself from within his fur until he had removed his T-shirt. He pushed it out from his collar.

Carol and Katherine were very surprised to see such a thing happening. But before they could ask about the thing emerging — some kind of dispensable organ? — Max had tied it to a stick and began to wave it above the bunker. And the barrage ended soon after.

Sensing it was safe, Max climbed from the bunker and was faced with the Bad Guys, all four of them, standing in the clearing, unhidden, surrounded by what seemed to be a thousand animals of all sizes, lined up like ammunition, waiting to be used in the battle. The Bad Guys were looking at Max with deeply confused expressions. They couldn't seem to figure out what Max was doing with the stick and the undershirt. Meanwhile, Max was trying to figure out how the enemy had gotten all those cats and dual-sided sheep to stand, still and docile, awaiting their inclusion in the war. It was impressive and Max intended to ask them about it later.

But for now he wanted to set forth a new set of rules. He put the flag down momentarily and stepped toward the Bad Guys. "Okay," he said. "There— "

The sentence went unfinished, as Alexander's arm swung and Max was hit in the mouth by a gelatinous ball of something. It knocked him flat on the ground. While he recovered, he got a look at and taste of the projectile — some kind of land-dwelling jellyfish, many-tentacled and many-limbed, that tasted bitter and medicinal. It got up and scurried off and then down an unseen hole.

Max got up. "Wait!" he said. "You can't— "

He was hit again, this time by a rock. Just a simple rock, thrown by Judith, which hit him in the stomach, knocking the wind out of him. He gasped, blurry eyed, doubled over, looking at his crown, which had fallen to the dirt. While he was struggling to find his next breath, the Bad Guys unleashed an incredible barrage of gelatinous balls, tiny cats, eight-legged mushrooms, and buffalo-seeming creatures. They fell all around him, and at least five more Larrys hit him, three of them in the nether region. He grabbed his crown and turned and ran, barely managing to make it to the bunker, where he collapsed on the ground, holding his lower self.

"Great war so far, King!" Carol said.

"Yeah," Douglas said. "Who's winning?"

Max lay on the ground, unable to speak. He also realized he'd left his undershirt on the battlefield, and now had no way to indicate ceasefire or surrender. After a few minutes, Max caught his breath and was able to ask, "Why didn't they stop?"

"Stop what?" Carol asked.

"The war."

"Why would they?" Carol asked.

Max explained the meaning of the white flag.

"Oh, I don't think they understood that," Carol said.

Katherine giggled. "We were all sitting here, *wondering* why you were doing that thing with the stick and the white thing. We thought it was some kind of weapon you were using, but then you got clobbered so bad that we figured, you know, it probably isn't a weapon, given how badly he's getting clobbered and all." She laughed till she couldn't breathe. Carol and Douglas joined in.

Max was losing his patience. He explained to his comrades that he was trying to explain to the enemy that they shouldn't throw animals during the war, and that rocks were too hard and could cause real injury, and that sticks might poke out one of their eyes. "They could cause *permanent damage*," he said, making sure that Katherine heard him.

She nodded seriously now. "So only *we* should use them. That makes sense."

"No, no!" Max said. "No one should."

His teammates contemplated this for a while, as more animals, rocks, and trees exploded around them.

"Wow, King," Douglas said. "I wish you'd explained all that to them before we got started. It'll be hard to get them to abide by the new rules now, with us being in the middle of a war and all."

Just then, Max saw that Alexander was making his way around the stand of trees, attempting — could it be? — to infiltrate their bunker. Or at least execute some kind of blindside attack. Thinking quickly, Max grabbed the biggest rock he could and gave it to Douglas.

"Get the goat!" he yelled.

In one fluid motion, Douglas wound up and unleashed a laser shot that sent the rock directly into Alexander's back, flattening him utterly.

"Wow, you have a good arm!" Max marveled. Douglas looked at his arm, as if he'd never really seen it before.

"Do it again!" he said, and Douglas threw another devastating blow at Alexander, who was still on the ground. This one hit him in the thigh, and made a very loud and painful-sounding thwack. Max really didn't like Alexander so much, and was happy to be avenged for the initial sneak attack that had started the whole battle.

"That's amazing!" Max said to Douglas. "You have the best arm around!"

Carol's head turned, and he gave Max a very surprised and then stern look. Max wasn't sure why and didn't have time to think about it because at that moment, Alexander began to get up. He was sniffling, wiping his nose, and maybe even crying. "You're not supposed to hit me in the back!" he yelled. "That wasn't fair!"

Now Judith's voice was heard: "Oh c'mon, Alexander. Don't cry. You can't cry in a war." Then there was a murmur of discussion between her and Ira. "Even Ira says you shouldn't cry in a war. Oh wait." She turned to Ira again, who whispered something in her ear. "Ira says you can sob, but you can't cry."

"I don't care what Ira says!" Alexander said. "He doesn't get to talk here!"

All this talk was boring Max, and Alexander's voice, more so than any voice he'd ever heard, made him want to muffle it. "Get him one more time," he told Douglas.

And Douglas threw a rock, this one bigger than the last two, and for a second it eclipsed Alexander's head completely. Then the goat was down, unmoving.

Max was very happy for a few seconds — because it was something to see, accuracy like that — and then, slowly, he began to feel kind of bad. Alexander still wasn't moving. Max's stomach clenched, thinking he'd ordered the actual killing of an actual goat-boy, but just then Alexander hopped up. He crossed his arms and made a series of nasty gestures to both Good Guys and Bad.

"I quit," he snarled, and walked off.

Max had to think about these latest developments. He hadn't liked getting hit by a rock — his stomach still ached from the rock Judith had thrown — but then again, when his team had used rocks on Alexander, it had caused him to surrender. Now the Bad Guys only had three soldiers left, which would make victory for

Max's team more likely. So now it made perfect sense. He was wrong to ban rocks, or even animals. The key was to use any or all weapons at one's disposal, but to just make sure you won when you used them. Max was sure that with Douglas's arm on their side, the Good Guys would prevail. And even if he did want to change the rules, and restrict the use of certain ammunition, he would have to find a way to make the Bad Guys listen. They hadn't responded to the white flag, so Max concluded that the only way to end all this would be first, to win, and to win in such a way that incapacitated the enemy so thoroughly that he would have the chance to tell them — if he decided to tell them at all — not to throw rocks and animals next time. Simple enough.

With this plan in mind, he formulated a strategy. They would retreat up to the hill behind them, and then unleash an all-out attack from above.

On Max's cue, they all abandoned their bunker and ran into the woods, and then climbed the hill.

The animal-artillery continued to land all around them, hitting the ground with thumps and squeals before hobbling off. There was so much squealing and grunting that when Douglas disappeared down a hole, letting out a quick shriek as he did so, none of Max's team members realized what had happened. Max and Carol and Katherine had taken shelter behind a large rock near the hole when they finally heard him.

"Hello?" Douglas called out.

"What happened?" Max asked.

"I think I fell down a hole," Douglas said.

Carol snapped his fingers. "I knew it! I was going to guess either that he fell down a hole or that he'd become invisible."

No one had any idea how to get him out. He was about twenty feet down.

Meanwhile, the animal-artillery fire was getting closer. Max knew that they needed to climb higher, to get out of range. He also knew that when they got high enough to mount a counterattack, they had to so thoroughly stun the enemy that his team would have enough time to save Douglas from the hole.

From deep in the earth, Douglas cleared his throat. "Oh, also, I think there's some kind of plant eating my left leg. So the sooner you can get me out, the better."

Max was standing above the hole, trying to figure out how they could get him out, when he was hit in the neck by something. Was it a rock? It felt like a rock. He looked down, and found that it was a snake, wrapped around a rock. The snake, noting that Max was the closest bitable thing, bit Max.

"Ah!" Max yelled.

Katherine looked at Max as if he'd just done something very impolite.

"Shhh," she said. "You'll hurt his feelings."

The snake slithered off, dejected.

"That wasn't nice," Katherine said. "It's not like it was a poison bite or anything."

Max was suddenly very worried. "Poison?"

"Wait a minute, maybe it *was* poison," she said, placing her chin in her hand. "I guess we'll know in a few more seconds. She stared at Max, examining his eyes and mouth. Finally satisfied, she smiled.

"Not poison. You'd have been dead by now. Good job getting bitten by the right kind of snake."

Thunk! Another rock, another actual rock, hit Max in the stomach, in the same spot as before. This time he wasn't sure who had thrown it, but it made him angrier than he'd ever been.

"Get up the hill!" Max commanded.

He and Carol and Katherine limped and crawled to the top of the hill, taking shelter behind a large boulder covered in the red-embroidery-looking moss he'd seen on his way to the fire the first night.

Max collapsed against the rock. His leg was going numb. His stomach was raw and throbbing. He wanted revenge, and soon. Now the plan seemed inevitable, and needed to be enacted immediately. On a personal level there was the need for some retribution, and on a more practical level, his team needed to smash the enemy sufficiently so that they could have time to save Douglas from the plant that was eating his leg at the bottom of the hole.

"We really need to get those guys," Max said. "I mean really kill 'em. Destroy 'em."

They discussed ways to do this, to kill and destroy the enemy, for a few minutes, until Max realized that at the top of the hill his team had no ammunition at all.

"All we have are these giant boulders covered in moss," Carol noted dejectedly.

"Yeah, and the river of lava flowing just under the surface," lamented Katherine.

Without much effort, Max was able to concoct a notion, which entailed his team lifting the boulders, soaking them in lava, and then rolling them down the hill to crush the enemy. He proposed it to his troops.

"Wow, that would really kill them," Carol said.

"It'll destroy them, too," Katherine added.

So they began.

Katherine ripped open a section of earth, revealing a slow river of lava. Max couldn't believe it — lava no more than four inches below the surface. He wanted to know everything about its hows and whys but there was no time just then.

Carol lifted a boulder and lowered it into the molten stream. Spinning it, he managed to cover the boulder in lava, which set the moss aflame.

"Now what, King?" he asked, looking slightly uncomfortable holding the white-hot boulder.

"Roll it at them," Max said.

And so Carol carried the lava-covered rock over to the edge of the hill, and tossed it in the direction of the Bad Guys. It rolled down the incline, gaining momentum as it went, knocking over trees, setting grass and bushes aflame, and letting loose countless rocks and gravel. By the time it approached the bottom, half the hill was on fire, and Judith and Ira and Alexander were screaming, because the flaming boulder, and the thousand or so smaller boulders and rocks it carried with it, were headed directly for them.

Max was torn at this point, because on the one hand, it was a pretty incredible sight. Seeing this kind of destruction unleashed, seeing a plan like this in action, and seeing it work so well — there was nothing in the world as good. On the other hand, it really looked like the Bad Guys would be crushed flat, and might actually be made dead, by the coming avalanche. He was suddenly very afraid.

"Hey," he said to his team, "you think they'll really get killed by that stuff?"

"Oh definitely," Katherine said.

"I hope so!" Carol said.

"What?" Max was aghast.

"I thought that was the point," Carol said, genuinely confused now.

As quickly as he could, Max explained that he didn't mean that he actually wanted them killed.

Carol was watching the avalanche, grinning and nodding, but still seemed perplexed. "So when you said, 'Let's kill them!' you meant, 'Let's beat them at this game by throwing dirt at them'?"

Max nodded.

"So we should prevent them from getting killed now?"

Max nodded.

"Okay," Carol said. Then he stood there for a long moment. "But how?"

The boulder continued down the hill, gaining speed.

"I told you not to do that," Katherine said.

"What?" Carol said. "You never said anything like that! You're the biggest liar in the world, Katherine."

"But you're the violent one," she said. "Too bad."

At that moment, the flaming lava boulder, and the thousands of accompanying rocks and flaming bushes — and even a pair of buffalo, who had been thrown up the hill as ammunition and were running down now, fleeing the juggernaut — struck and mowed over the Bad Guys. There seemed to be no possibility at all they could have survived.

CHAPTER XXXIV

"I can't feel it so well," Douglas said, holding his half-chewed leg, which looked, after being gnawed on by some kind of carnivorous underground vine, a lot like a piece of black licorice. "Not that I'm complaining."

It was later, dark, and they were all around a small fire. All of the beasts were trying as best they could to recover from the war, and were waiting sullenly to eat something Douglas had prepared — a victory dinner, he was calling it. Even though his leg had been partially devoured, he was in a bright mood, high on the compliment Max, the king, had paid his heretofore unnoticed arm.

Alexander stared at Max. "That was a dumb idea."

"I'm still sort of hollow," Ira moaned. "My eyeballs feel loose..."

"Quiet Ira," Judith snapped. "Everyone's eyeballs feel loose. I can barely feel my brain. Can anyone feel their brain?"

No one answered. No one could feel their brains.

Without a word, the Bull came to Max, took the crown from his head, and put it in the center of the fire. As before, Max didn't want to question the tradition, though he really didn't like seeing his crown there, under the flames.

Max's head was a muddle. Maybe he hadn't thought the war through. It had seemed like simple fun when he had first pictured it, with a glorious beginning, a difficult but valor-filled middle, and a victorious end. He hadn't accounted for the fact that there might not be much of a resolution to the battle, and he hadn't imagined what it would feel like when the war just sort of ended, without anyone admitting defeat and congratulating him for his bravery. Instead, Judith and Ira had been thrown off the cliff, and Katherine and Carol had gotten angrier at each other, and Alexander wasn't talking to Ira, because somehow in his mind it was Ira's fault that Alexander had gotten hit so many times with rocks. Meanwhile, the Bull was now sitting off to the side of the fire, dirt everywhere on him. He had walked straight through the battlefield all day, absorbing hundreds of blows, without ever ducking or running. Other than the scrapes and dust, though, his appearance hadn't changed much. If anything, he seemed more alive, more likely to talk.

"So Max," Judith said. "Was this what you had in mind, or did I misunderstand something? You get to the island, declare yourself king, and then try to get us killed half a dozen ways? Was that the idea?"

"Judith, stop," Carol said firmly. "Everyone was trying

to kill everyone. Don't flatter yourself. Besides, I'm sure Max has it figured out."

Carol looked to Max and gave him a warm smile. Max tried to smile back, but he was still having trouble squaring the gentle Carol he knew and admired with the Carol who hadn't felt the least hesitation with seeing his friends flattened by flaming boulders. Max was feeling chopped up inside. Never before had such a disaster so undebatably been his fault. He had brought up the war, and half of the participants had nearly died. It seemed to Max that everything he did, at home or here on this island, caused permanent damage. And Katherine, who alone seemed capable of really listening to him, was nowhere to be found.

"Food's almost done," Douglas said, strutting around with his right arm half-flexed, as if hoping for another affirmation of his extraordinary limb.

"Close your eyes, Max," he said.

Max closed his eyes.

"I made a surprise for you. Your first royal meal."

Max could smell something being put under his nose. His body shook involuntarily. It was the most potent and wretched smell he had ever encountered. It was like a thousand long-dead fish soaked in gasoline and eggs.

"Okay, now you can look," Douglas said.

Max opened his eyes.

He almost jumped. It was a huge snake. Or a worm. About a foot in diameter. Wet and brown and purple, about eleven feet long. Douglas had placed it on Max's lap.

"Don't worry. We killed him," Douglas said. He laughed. "You thought it was still alive! That's funny."

Max stood up, letting the worm roll off his lap. A thick brown and green residue remained on his white fur.

"Something wrong, King?" Douglas asked.

Max tried to mask his horror.

"No, no!" he said, then found the appropriate answer. "I just wanted to get a better look at it."

Douglas smiled. "Yeah, I got him out of the lagoon. He was sort of wrapping himself around Judith, so I dove down and grabbed him. He's probably lived there for a hundred years! And now you get to eat him!"

Douglas was staring at Max, searching for signs of approval. Max tried to smile.

"You can eat the mouth if you want," Douglas said. "That's the part with the most texture."

Max's stomach was sliding down his legs. He had to come up with a reason he wasn't going to eat the worm.

He looked around, finding no answers in the dirt or trees, but when he raised his eyes to the sky, he found the solution.

"I'm afraid I can't eat this dinner tonight. I thank you very much, but the kings where I come from don't eat on nights without stars."

The beasts accepted this — "Oh", "Too bad for you", "Kings have it rough" — they said, and began to eat. They grabbed at the wet flesh of the giant worm with their claws, the bloody juice pouring down their chins and between their fingers. Max couldn't watch. He stared at the fire.

And as they ate it, the worm, Max soon realized, was causing different reactions in different beasts. Ira became quiet and melancholy, his eyes welling as he thought of some distant sweet memory. Douglas tried to fight the effects, his eyes darting around as his mouth went slack and his words began to slur. As for Judith, she became flirty, touching everyone on the arm, the shoulders, giggling and finding a half-dozen reasons to get up and find her way to Douglas so she could touch the back of his neck. But when he slapped her paw away for the last time, her sharper edges appeared again, and she narrowed her eyes at Max.

"I can't believe we're still not talking about what's on everyone's mind," Judith said. "The king here is trying to kill off some of us. Is that of concern to anyone?"

No one answered, but it was obvious that the subject was on the minds of at least half the beasts.

"So Max sailed for over a year!" Carol offered, intent on changing the subject.

"That's a long time," Douglas said cheerfully.

"A whole year alone," Ira said, looking up into the darkness. "That's so sad."

"Why'd it take that long, King? Slow boat?" Judith asked, her eyes full of menace.

"No, it was a good boat," Max said.

"So you're just not a good sailor?" she taunted.

"No, I'm a really good sailor. I mean, the boat didn't have a motor on it. I was sailing as fast as that boat…"

"Oh, I'm just giving you a hard time," Judith giggled, without any mirth at all. "Don't be so sensitive! Really though, have we already experienced the full range of your plans for fixing everything on the island? A parade, a war, and then we all die from molten lava?"

Carol stared Judith down. Finally she looked away and continued eating.

"I'm feeling the void again," Ira added.

"Don't worry, Ira," Douglas said. "Max'll solve it. He always says the right things. Just wait. Right Max? Go ahead."

Everyone stared at Max, and Max was surprised to see that their faces were genuinely hopeful, expectant. There was real hope that Max, their king, truly did have a notion.

"Well, I thought…" Max mumbled. He didn't, actually, have another plan at all. The silence stretched out uncomfortably. Finally he arrived at an idea, though its quality was uncertain. "I thought… I thought I could give you all royal titles."

Ira looked confused.

Judith cleared her throat.

Alexander snickered.

No one was impressed, not even Carol. The look on his face was more like shock. He couldn't believe that was the best Max could do. Max tried to spruce up the plan:

"…and I could give you all special duties and, like, those things that go across your chest," he said, while gesturing in a diagonal across his torso, trying to remember the word for *sash*.

"Snakes?" Judith guessed.

"No…" Max said.

"We already have snakes," Judith said.

"No, no…" Max insisted.

"I don't like wearing snakes there," Ira said.

"It's not a snake!" Max snapped. "It's more royal than that. It's— "

"A stick?" Douglas said, trying to help.

"No!" Max wailed.

"Sounds like a snake to me," Judith said. "And no one likes to wear snakes there— "

"Let me finish!" Max barked.

Max tried to think of the word. "It's…" he meandered, gesturing across his chest again. "It's…"

Finally he gave up, defeated. "You'll have royal titles," he mumbled.

The silence was profound. Max's subjects were so underwhelmed that they didn't need to say anything. Max had to move onward and upward as soon as he could, so he stood, thinking he knew what to do. It had cheered his mom up, it had made his sister and her friends laugh hysterically — it would have to work here. He made his arms and legs stiff and began his incredible robot dance.

But as he did the dance — and he did it very well, as good as ever before — the beasts, far from being impressed, were alarmed.

"What's he doing?" Judith asked. "What is that?"

"Uh oh, somebody broke the king," Ira concluded.

"Is he sick?" Judith wondered aloud.

"I don't know, but it's making *me* sick," Alexander grumbled. "What kind of king would do something like this?"

Max gave up. He stopped dancing. The beasts seemed greatly relieved to see him sit down again.

"I think he's done now," Ira noted.

"I hope so," Alexander said.

"What just happened?" Judith asked.

"I was doing a robot," Max explained. "You're supposed to laugh."

No one had laughed. No one was smiling now.

"What's a robot?" Ira said. He sounded scared.

"A robot?" Max said. "A robot?"

No one knew what a robot was.

"C'mon, a *robot*," Max said. "Robots are the best."

"What's that?" Carol said sharply.

"Robots are the best," Max repeated, less sure now.

Carol seemed genuinely taken aback.

"That's what we waited for?" Alexander said. "Pathetic."

"Did that kind of thing work the last place you were king?" Judith asked.

Douglas furrowed his brow. The Bull's stare was oppressive. Even Carol looked disappointed in Max, profoundly so.

"I'm getting hungry," Alexander said, staring intensely at Max.

Carol could see where this was headed.

"You just ate," Carol growled. "No one's hungry."

Judith glared at Max and licked her lips. "Everyone's hungry and you know it."

Carol stood, imposing his figure over the group. "No. No one's hungry. Now get up. Let's go," he said. The beasts stared at him, as if sizing him up anew — had he lost any strength? Was he vulnerable in any new way? After a moment, it seemed that no, no one could yet challenge his primacy. They all began to stand and prepared to go.

At that moment, a snowflake appeared. Then more

— the snow fell in drunken spirals. Douglas's admiration for Max had faded, and now he looked at Max in an ugly way. "Good thing you destroyed our homes, King."

Alexander was happy to heap on the scorn. "Thanks, Your Heinous. I mean Your Highness."

Judith, Alexander, and Ira walked off. Douglas soon followed, shaking his head. As he left the campground he paused, wanting to say something to Max, but unsure just what that something would be.

Carol waited for everyone to leave. He was on the other side of the fire, looking at his hands.

"Robots are the best, huh? I thought I— "

"That's not what I meant," Max said. "I didn't mean they were better than *you*."

"But you said they were the *best*. Who are they, anyway? Are they bigger than me? Stronger? I don't know how that could be possible."

"They're not," Max said. "You're the biggest. By far."

"Then why'd you say they were the best? That means you think they're better. I mean, forget it. There's no reason to talk about it. What's said is said."

Max was lost. He was so tired and confused he didn't know what to say. He stared at the ground for a moment, and when he looked up, Carol was crouched down, his ear to the earth.

"I don't like the sound of this," he said. "It's loud and it's scrambled and it's very angry."

Carol turned to leave the campsite.

"Night, Max. I guess you have a lot to figure out tonight. Good luck." With that, he disappeared into the woods.

Max heard a crackle of twigs breaking. He turned to see the Bull, gigantic and menacing, standing behind him. They stared at each other. Neither blinked. Then, without a sound, the Bull turned and walked away into the night.

Max was alone. The fire was dwindling, it was snowing lightly, he was on an island in the middle of the sea, and he was alone.

CHAPTER XXXV

All night Max stared into the fire, cold and rattled as the snow continued to fall. He found logs and added them, scooting closer to the flames, trying to stay warm.

Max had to put order to his thoughts, had to straighten out his quail. He started with what he knew, cataloguing what he had learned so far. He knew that Douglas liked having his arm praised as being the best, but he knew that Carol didn't like hearing that kind of praise directed at someone other than himself, and he certainly didn't like being told that robots were the best, because presumably, he considered himself the best. He knew that Katherine preferred to be alone with Max. He knew that Judith and Alexander and Ira did not like getting run over by boulders covered in lava and that the possibility of grave injury likely reminded Ira of the void, even the thought of which was to be averted at all costs.

He knew he wanted food. He was nearly delirious with

hunger. His head felt light, his stomach jagged. And what he wanted, more than any other food, was soup. Soup would go down easy, would warm and soften everything within him. Any kind of soup would do, but cream of mushroom soup, which his mother made for him when he was feeling sick, would be best.

Maybe, he thought, he should go home. He wasn't sure that sailing home was even possible, because the continent he'd come from seemed to have disappeared altogether a few hours after he'd left its shore, but he certainly could try. And if he didn't make it there, there were surely other islands, with other animals or people he could lord over.

But even if he could make it home, he was sure his family had forgotten him. He'd been gone for days, and by now they would assume he was dead and gone, and they would likely be happy for it. Maybe the house had fallen in on itself from all the damage he'd done to it. Maybe his mother and sister had been crushed under the weight of the beams he'd weakened with all that water. No, no, he convinced himself. They were alive, but happy to be rid of an animal like him.

He thought again of going where he'd meant to go in the first place, to his dad's apartment in the city. He could still do it. If he sailed south-southwest, he would have to get there eventually. And once he got there, he could live there, and he knew how happy his dad would be to have him.

The first problem would be the bed. His dad only had the one bed, and it wasn't so big, so Max usually slept on the fold-out in the den, and the mattress was thin and the joints of the couch-bed creaked. The room was cold and the sounds of the street were loud and unpredictable. All night there were bursts from the never-sleeping city: sirens and arguments, cackling laughter, bottles shattering in Dumpsters, the hissing of trucks. And when his dad had company over, there were other sounds, too.

Her name was Pamela.

She was pretty in a loud way, with big green eyes and a wide glossy mouth. She worked at a restaurant or owned it or something and they had eaten there, the first time Max had ever sat at a table at a place like that, with a candle in the middle and the whole place amber-colored and dim. It was so boring he wanted to scream.

Pamela had ordered food for all of them, a succession of small dishes, greasy and mud-colored, and Max had ended up eating little but bread. Max's dad had given him imploring looks, but Max knew he wouldn't yell at him for not eating, not in front of Pamela.

Afterward she took them down to a basement full of bottles and finally Max was intrigued. He wanted to own that place. Not for the bottles, but for all the wooden shelves, the cubbies, the arched doorways and dark corners. It was like a castle, a dungeon, the labyrinth underneath an ancient kingdom. But for Pamela it was just a place to keep wine. She pulled two dark bottles from the wall and they went up the stairs.

After dinner the three of them took a taxi back to his dad's building. At the front door, she had said goodbye to Max and Max's dad, but then there had been some whispering, a quick giggle, and she'd walked off, around the corner, a bottle in each hand.

Max was put to bed, but couldn't sleep. He lay awake, thinking about the labyrinth under the restaurant, how safe he felt there within its stone walls, its cool dark solidity, until he heard the door squeal open and the drop of two shoes. The sound of bottles clinking together, followed by a volley of shushes. Then footsteps shrinking down the hallway and the closing of his father's door.

Max couldn't go to his father's apartment. He couldn't sail there, he couldn't sail home, and the probability of finding and becoming king of another island seemed remote. He had to try to make this one work. How hard could it be to tame this place and please everyone at all times?

Max awoke in the night, his shoulders shaking. He had fallen asleep before feeding the fire properly, and now it was gone. The snow had stopped and the night was black. He couldn't see a thing in any direction, just vague patches of grey where snow had gathered. He put a handful in his mouth to quench his thirst but he knew he was in trouble. With the temperature dropping and no way to make or find fire, he could easily freeze this night. If he walked in any direction he would be eaten or stung or fall down some interminable hole. He couldn't go anywhere.

And finally he cried. When the tears came, they felt so good. His chest shook, and the hot tears warmed his face, and he laughed at how good it all felt. They kept coming, so many tears, one for every frustration and fear he'd known since he left home. Oh man, he thought, this feels so good. He loved the hot tears, the release of it all. He loved that he could do it here, alone, in the blackness, unseen by anyone. He could cry as much as he wanted and no one would ever know.

He cried for what felt like hours but the crying and shaking and slurping up great amounts of mucus served to somehow keep him warm as the early hours grew colder, and the tears and the cold and everything he'd been thinking about combined to form in his mind something like an idea. And the idea told him to get a stick, and his hand began to move the stick around the dirt and ash, and before long he had drawn up a notion that had a chance to do everything that needed to be done for him and every other beast of the island: it would fill the void, it would eliminate the chatter, it would connect everything and everyone that had been unconnected, and it would, best of all, ensure that never again would he sleep in the snow, without a fire, alone on an island in the middle of the sea.

CHAPTER XXXVI

Much of the snow that fell the night before had now melted. Max's vision was blurry as he woke up amid the pre-dawn light. His wolf suit was filthy. But he was so excited he had spent most of the night awake, waiting for the first blue light so he could find Carol and announce to him and the rest of the beasts that he knew how to change everything, once and for all.

When it was light enough for him to navigate his way to Carol's perch on the high dunes, Max picked his crown from the ashes of the fire and put it on. It was still hot, and he flinched from the heat, but he steeled himself and headed to the sea.

When the forest gave way to the beach, Max could see that all the beasts were there, on the snow-dusted sand, and that they had slept there. It was probably the coldest place on the island that anyone might have chosen to spend the night.

Max found Carol sitting alone, on his high dune, facing the horizon. Max ran toward him.

"Carol!"

This woke up Judith and Ira, each of them wearing a thin blanket of snow. They watched Max pass by.

"Carol!" Max yelled.

Carol was still facing away, staring intensely at the sea. And just like the previous morning, just as the wet orange sun rose from the horizon, he heaved a great sigh of relief and turned around.

"Oh hey. Hi Max," he said.

"Carol, I have an idea. I know what we're going to do."

"Good, good, Max. What's the plan?"

CHAPTER XXXVII

Carol gathered everyone around and they found a good flat spot on the sand for Max to draw his plans. With a stick he recreated the sketch he'd worked on throughout the night. When he was done, it looked just like he'd envisioned and, though a bit crude, it was grand enough to convince anyone, he thought.

"What is that?" Judith asked. Ira was laying below her, chewing on her calf and drooling profusely.

"It's a fort," Max said.

"What's a fort?" she asked. "And why is a fort better than, say, me eating your head?"

"It's way better than that," Max said. "It'll be the ultimate fort of all time. It'll be part castle, part mountain, and part ship…" He glanced at Carol and corrected himself. "Except it won't sail, because it's stationary. It's definitely stationary.

"Yeah," Max went on, "it's gonna be as tall as twelve

of you and six of me. It'll be big enough to fit everyone inside. We'll be able to sleep in a big pile like we did the first night."

Carol and Douglas nodded respectfully.

Ira now had the whole of Judith's lower leg in his mouth, but removed it long enough to say, "Hmm."

"And it'll make us feel good," Max added, for Judith's benefit. "All the time."

"What will?" Judith said.

"The fort," Max said.

"No it won't," she said. "Why would a fort for *you* make us happy? What about eating? That makes me happy."

"Judith. Shh. Listen," Douglas said.

"It's not just *my* fort," Max said. "We'll build it together. It'll be all of us on one team."

Judith seemed almost impressed. "Oh. *That* kind of fort."

"Yeah, and inside we'll have everything we could ever want. We'll have our own detective agency, and our own language. Alexander, do you want to be in charge of making up a new language?"

"No," Alexander said.

"Okay, I'll work on the language," Max said, forging ahead. "And outside I want to have lots of ladders. And stained glass. And there'll be a fake tree outside, but it's not a tree, it's a tunnel, and it'll lead you inside, through a compartment..."

Max drew the tree outside the fort, but the Bull's toe was on the beach, where the tree needed to be. Max drew half the tree and ran up against the Bull's toe. He looked up to the Bull, but it was clear the Bull wasn't going to move. So Max drew around the huge toe, such that the round head of the tree became a half-moon. The half-moon reminded Max of something. The fort needed tunnels. Lots of tunnels.

"Ira, will you be in charge of the tunnels?" Max asked. "They're like holes, and you can make holes, right?"

"Yeah, I make holes," he said.

"Okay, these tunnels need to be the longest holes known to man. And while you're down there digging you can also make a basement, the biggest one of all time, where we'll have a million games for when it's raining."

The beasts all nodded, listening intently, as if looking at a series of specific and reasonable instructions. Douglas made notations on his arm.

"We'll have a huge turret for the owls," Max continued. "We have to have lots of owls because they have good eyes and they don't get scared. And we'll train them and guide them with remote control. They'll look out for invaders."

"I know some owls," Katherine said.

Everyone looked over to see that Katherine had been there for some time.

"Good, good," Max said.

"Are these nice owls, or will they be aloof and judgmental?" Carol asked, giving Katherine a look askance.

"They're not aloof and judgmental," she answered, quiet but firm. "They're good owls. They care. They just don't know how to express it."

Carol softened. "Okay. We'll need some good owls."

An electric current seemed to flow through the group, as everyone, from Max to Douglas to Ira and Judith, recognized that they had just witnessed a silent, unsigned-but-still-significant truce between Carol and Katherine.

"It'll be us against everyone else," Max continued, now with extra vigor. "No one that we don't want in there can get in there."

"And it'll keep out the chatter, right Max?" Carol asked, almost rhetorically.

"Of course. How could chatter get in a place like this?" Max said, indicating the incredible size and strength of the fort as drawn with his stick in the sand.

Judith walked around the drawing, still skeptical.

"So what do you think?" Max asked her.

"I don't really think anything like this ever works," she said, "but if it *did* work…" she said, her voice rising to something like hopeful. "I don't know," she said, sitting down again. "I don't know anything. But I *do* like the tree tunnel."

"Best of all," Max said, looking to everyone, "we'll all sleep together in a real pile. Like we did before."

There was a general murmur of approval for this particular aspect of the proposal.

Now Max turned to Carol. "Will you be in charge of building it?"

Carol was taken aback. "Me? Oh. Huh. Well. I… I just…"

Douglas spoke up: "You should definitely be in charge, Carol. No one else could pull it off."

"Yeah, yeah. I know," Carol said, his pride lifting him. "You're right…"

"Don't you think Carol should build it, Katherine?" Max said.

"Yeah," she said, surprising everyone. "No one else can do it."

"Okay," Carol said finally. "Then I'll do it."

CHAPTER XXXVIII

Construction began immediately and proceeded with remarkable speed. Carol measured the perimeter of the fort using Ira as the primary unit of measurement — he and Douglas carried him like a giant ruler — and soon the entire foundation had been built of rocks and mud.

The Bull was collecting boulders and trees, throwing them hundreds of yards from wherever he was to the fort site. Building materials were piling up.

By midday the first wall went up, straight and tall, easily thirty feet.

"Wow, this is almost fun, King," Judith said, and then seemed confused about her own positive attitude. She went away muttering and counting on her fingers.

Douglas strutted by, alive with purpose. "Not bad, King," he said to Max. "You and Carol together — you plan a smart fort."

Even Alexander seemed to be enjoying himself. He

was finding and packing the mud that held the walls together, and he took great pride in the messy work.

Max found Ira below. "Nice digging!" Max said, genuinely impressed. In just a few hours Ira had already dug a basement bigger than Max's one at home, and the beginnings of the secret exit tunnels.

"Thanks, King. You know, I've never really thought about it, but basements are kind of like holes, except they're covered. You really like it so far?"

"Yeah, it's good," Max said.

"It's not too crumbly on the side or curvy, uh, on the bottom?"

"No, no. It's just right."

"Oh good. Good. I'm really glad," Ira said, beginning to dig again. "I'm glad I'm digging for you, Max."

The activity continued throughout the afternoon. Rocks were stacked, vines were woven, Douglas and Judith sank posts into the earth and stomped on them, pogo-style, to drive them deeper.

As the sun headed downward, the structure, though still skeletal, really was starting to look like Max's drawing, for better and worse. It was a bit crooked here and there — and Carol had been strangely faithful to the half-moon entrance Max had made when drawing around the Bull's foot — but in all it was an astonishing sight.

Max climbed a nearby ridge to get a better look at the construction. The fort was about eighty feet high already, and was climbing rapidly.

"What do you think, King?" It was Carol, who had

come up from behind Max. He, too, was surveying the progress from afar.

"It's amazing," Max said. "I just can't believe how big it is."

"Is it too big?" Carol asked, suddenly concerned.

"No, no," Max said, "it's perfect. I was just surprised now that it's real and everything. It's exactly right. You're doing a great job. The best."

Carol beamed.

When night came the beasts were exhausted, happily so. They gathered in the main room of the fort-to-be, for a celebratory feast. Again they chose to eat something inedible to Max — it looked suspiciously like seal — and again he sat and watched them eat, his own stomach roaring with hunger.

"You know, I really think we're onto something here," Douglas said, sitting back after gorging himself. "I think this is the one that really might work."

There was general agreement that Douglas had spoken the truth. And Max, hungry as he was, was very happy. His plan had worked, everyone was content, and they were sitting in a real circle, before a warm fire, in the fort he had designed himself, with a stick in the sand.

As he was recounting the day to himself, its many highlights, a sound began to weave itself into the night air. It sounded like a stringed instrument, a cello maybe, round and resonant and full. Max looked up, but no one was surprised or curious. No one else found it unusual.

Then he found Katherine, lying with her head on

Judith's thigh, her mouth open to the sky. The sound, some kind of singing, was coming from her. And soon others joined in. Judith was first, her sound sharper, coarser, but beautiful nonetheless — it seemed to circle and intersect with Katherine's voice in perfect harmony. One by one the others sent their voices up to weave with the rest, each sound complementing and deepening the whole. It was the prettiest music Max had ever heard, and the fact that it could exist, that it could be made by these lumbering animals, seemed to render small and forgettable any problems that had ever existed among them.

CHAPTER XXXIX

"Max."

A whisper.

"Max!"

A female voice.

Max had been asleep, using Carol's arm for a pillow, when he opened his eyes to see Katherine, crouched beside him.

"We need to get the owls," she whispered.

"Now?" Max asked.

"Yeah, this is the only time," she said, glancing at Carol to make sure he hadn't been woken. "Now!"

Max felt duty-bound to get the owls, essential for the protection of the kingdom. So he got up, careful not to wake Carol or anyone, and jogged after Katherine, who was already at the doorway to the fort. The sun was newly risen, and just as Max was realizing that this was the first morning Carol hadn't felt the need to sit waiting for the sun's arrival, Katherine lifted Max and threw him on her back.

"Grab my scruff," she said.

Max did, and Katherine immediately leapt from the fort area, landing first in the many-colored meadow, then atop one of her striped treetop platforms, and then in a forest of pink translucent plants, each time touching the ground with the speed and delicacy of a hummingbird.

They saw parts of the island Max didn't know existed — an area of high yellow grass populated by walking snakes, snakes who stood on hind legs of some kind, living in a clearing with a dozen geysers spouting bright orange plumes of sparks and mist. Finally they landed on the far side of the island, on a wide white beach with high dunes and corkscrew rock formations, cerulean blue, jutting every-where from the sand.

"Do you like it?" Katherine asked.

Max nodded. He loved it.

"I come here when I want to be alone," Katherine said. "I have to come here to remember who I am and who I'm not. See them?"

Katherine pointed up and Max saw two birds, red dots in the sky, flying in ellipses, then figure eights, crossing in perfect time. Max was hypnotized by the symmetry of their flight.

"Are those the owls?" he asked, hushed.

"Are those the owls?" Katherine repeated, mimicking him. "Of course they are. They're not seals. Everyone ate the last ones for dinner last night."

Before Max could think of a witty comeback, and just

as the thought of real seals being eaten by his friends had sunk in, he saw one of the owls plummet. It had been hit by a rock, thrown by Katherine, and so a red blur fell, almost straight down, from the sky. Max watched in horror, frozen, not wanting to see the bird crash into the earth but unable to look away.

But just as it approached the ground he saw that Katherine was there, underneath, waiting nonchalantly for its arrival. She caught the owl like an outfielder would a pop fly. Without waiting a beat and while cradling the first owl in her arm, Katherine threw another rock into the air, it connected with a second owl, and this one followed the same course as the first — it fell precipitously. Katherine monitored its flightpath and caught it with great care.

With an owl under each arm, she jogged over to where Max had stood paralyzed, watching.

"Here they are!" she said. "Aren't they great?"

Max wasn't sure what to say. They were magnificent birds, with crimson plumage and great auburn wings, but they seemed disoriented and damaged from being knocked from the sky by Katherine's rocks. Their pupils were spinning like tiny carousels. As if reading Max's thoughts, she reassured him.

"They don't feel it at all. Their bones and wings and everything are built to, uh, you know, make them not feel it when rocks hit them when I throw them," she said. Now she grabbed them each by their talons and swung them upside-down. "See? There's no damage at all. They love it, actually."

Max wasn't sure how this was being demonstrated by hanging them upside-down, but he was too confused to argue, and besides, what did he know about the health and welfare of sea owls?

"Let's sit down and rest for a second," Katherine said, plopping herself on a high dune.

Max wanted to get back to the fort site, to help with its construction and generally oversee things, but Katherine was in no hurry.

"Hey Max, do you like being carried?"

Max had no idea what this meant, but when he thought about it, being carried sounded like fun. It had been fun when he'd ridden on everyone's shoulders during the parade. "Yeah," he said.

"Yeah, me, too! We're so similar!" Katherine said, placing her hair behind her ear excitedly. "But this one time, I got a carrying monkey," she said, making a gesture as if holding a baby. "I got him for Carol, so he wouldn't have to walk all the way to his studio. It's so far, and I didn't want him to be tired before he even gets there. And everyone likes to be carried, right?"

"Yeah," Max said.

"Okay, right," Katherine continued, "so I gave him a monkey and then when he carried Carol I laughed and said I was surprised the monkey was strong enough. But then Carol got offended because he thought I meant that he was *fat* or something. But I was *joking*! So he said, 'Well, if I'm so fat I guess I should eat this monkey.' And then you know what he did? He *ate* the carrying monkey! Can you believe that?"

Max couldn't believe it.

"I don't know," she added, shaking her head. "He makes me think I can't do anything right."

They sat for a while, as Max tried to piece together what he'd just heard.

"Sorry to burden you with my issues," she said, then brightened. "Hey, let's make a wish."

In one deft motion with her claw, she peeled a layer of dune away. Max knelt down next to her and watched. Just a few inches under the surface, she revealed lava flowing just as it did atop the hill, glowing red and oozing downhill, underground, very slowly. A few flames jumped out and onto the sand. Max backed up. Katherine laughed.

She grabbed a cerulean pebble and gave one to Max. "Think of something you want."

Max closed his eyes tight, then nodded.

"Okay, now throw it in," she said.

Max threw his pebble in, watching as it was quickly subsumed with a little spark.

Katherine closed her eyes, making a wish before throwing her own rock in. She covered the trench up again, replacing the sand and stamping it down with her foot.

"You know what I wished for?" she asked. "I wished that you'll always be king. Is that what you wished for?"

Max nodded, but something was on his mind and he couldn't force it away.

"But wait," he asked. "He ate the carrying monkey?"

"Oh yeah," Katherine said, nodding vigorously. "He's eaten almost every gift I've given him."

"How big of a monkey was it?"

"You know, like a normal carrying monkey," she said, holding her arm up at the exact height of Max. "And it was really sudden."

Registering Max's shock, Katherine brightened. "Wow, I sound like a downer, don't I! Don't worry. That's not what I wanted *at all*. Let's head back."

CHAPTER XL

That night, as the fort neared completion, the beasts ate together again, this time feasting on the huge flat feet of some animal Max hadn't even seen intact and now wanted no part of devouring. Afterward they all collapsed in exhaustion and gluttony, arranged in an interlocking chain of limbs and torsos, circling the dimming fire.

They all fell quickly to sleep, but Max was awake, thinking of monkeys being eaten in one quick bite. Since his morning with Katherine he had thought of little else. Though the afternoon had been full of triumph — the walls were all assembled, the staircases had been built, the basement finished and covered, the tunnels dug in every direction for escape from any and all calamity — Max was stricken with the idea that he could be just as easily eaten as a carrying monkey, and at any time.

Would Carol do such a thing? He had seen flashes of his anger, had been surprised when he was willing to actually kill his enemies on the field of fake-battle. It was one thing to fear the devouring of the rest of the beasts, for Max always had Carol to protect him. But if Carol himself decided to eat him, his head and arms and legs, what would stop him?

Max had been among creatures so much bigger than him for so long that he had to fear, in some small way, for his life more or less at all times. It was just a matter of proportion, really. It wasn't that they were always meaning to harm him — though they had threatened to eat him many times — but they had also, mistakenly or carelessly, almost maimed or murdered him a half-dozen other times. He had nearly been knocked off a cliff, had been pelted with hairless buffalo, and had almost been crushed by rolling beast-boulders.

He could spend a lot of time, now or in the future, trying to figure out what motivated them all — why they did certain things he wished they didn't do, and didn't do other things he wished they would. The creatures were often doing confusing things when he stumbled upon them: he would be running through the forest, looking for something to do, when he would see Judith's back, and perhaps the side of Ira. And then he would see Ira's hand inside Judith's ear, and Judith's left foot tapping quickly, and the both of them humming intensely. "Oh, hi King," they would say, and Ira would immediately remove his hand from Judith's ear and the humming and tapping would cease. He found Douglas more than once sitting alone near the chalky cliffs, moaning and rocking and once even punching himself in the head.

And as Max was contemplating all this, a scraping sound came from Carol's direction. Max looked over to find him in the middle of his own restless dream. He clawed the ground with his talons, creating deep grooves in the dirt. Max watched as Carol whimpered, growled, and bared his teeth menacingly, all while asleep. Suddenly, Carol, in the middle of some nightmare, lunged toward Max, his claws coming within inches of Max's face. Max gasped and recoiled. He backed up, crab-style, until he was nestled into Katherine, who murmured something welcoming. As Max burrowed deeper into Katherine, Carol continued to grab and groan and Max continued to watch, wide-eyed, from the shadows.

CHAPTER XLI

The morning sky was paper-white and low. Max was inside the fort, pacing out dimensions, drawing an outline on the floor. Carol approached and immediately took notice of Max's markings. "What's that?"

Max hadn't expected to have to tell Carol about this idea so soon. He knew it might upset Carol, but there was no going back, and he didn't want to lie.

"Well..." Max said, "I was thinking that we need to put a... a place inside where the king is secret. Like a secret chamber for the king."

Carol looked at the fort, tilting his head.

"A secret what? I don't understand."

"Well," Max said, adopting the air of an experienced architect of castles and kingdoms, "all kingdoms have a special place for the king, where there's a door and a key... Like a small place." Max indicated a space just big enough for himself.

"So just big enough for you?" Carol said, as if the notion was beyond preposterous.

"Exactly," Max said, "the king needs some time to be alone, in a little place... All kings have something like that. It's... It's where they come up with their best plans to make everything good for everyone."

Carol thought about this for a second. "A small place... Okay, okay. Interesting. But how would *we* get in?"

"Well, I'd let you in."

"But the door you drew is too small."

"Yeah, that's the best part. The door will be secret. And very small. Just big enough for me."

As Carol began to understand the implications of the secret door, his expression clouded over. "I don't know," he said, studying the fort, "I didn't picture it with secret doors. Secret doors don't belong in this fort."

"But it's my fort, isn't it?" Max said. "I mean, I'm the king, right?"

"Yeah, of course," Carol said, deflated. "I just need a second to wrap my head around the idea." He turned from the doors, then turned back again. "And you'll let us in..." He thought more about it, staring at the wall as if his eyes might bore straight through. "But what if it's a *big* place with a secret door?"

"No, no. That's not how it would be done," Max insisted. "It should be— "

Carol punched a hole in the wall, leaving a fist-sized gap.

"About *that* big?" Carol seethed.

"Yeah."

"Fine."

His shoulders tense with rage, Carol walked outside and found Douglas.

"Hey Douglas, we're gonna need a new room in the middle here, a small one with a secret door. The main doors are the same but the doors here are gonna be secret."

Douglas studied the structure for a moment. He was not pleased with having to redo his work, and he knew that Max's directive was not pleasing to Carol.

With a sigh, Douglas made his announcement to everyone. "Okay everyone — there's a little room in the middle and the door's gonna be secret!"

There were murmurs of confusion throughout the site. Douglas repeated the directive, now louder: "The door's gonna be secret! The door's gonna be secret!"

CHAPTER XLII

"Psst. Come here," came a voice. Max turned around to see Judith.

Max stepped over to Judith, who had just emerged from a hole in the ground — the fake tree tunnel. Ira was next to her, chewing quietly on her arm.

"Secret doors, huh?" she said, her head tilted, her eyes squinted. "You know, I've been watching you. And just yesterday I thought you had really saved us, but now I see what's happening. And it's really interesting to see you work."

Judith stared at Max, not paying the least bit of attention to Ira, who was gnawing with increasing intensity on her arm. Max didn't know what she was talking about.

"You're really manipulative, you know that?" she said. "Do you know what that word means?"

"Yeah," Max said, though he didn't.

"No you don't," she said. "It means the ability to find

the exact opportune moment, and the exact way, to get someone to do what you want them to do."

"I didn't do that," Max snapped.

"But look how you made Carol feel. Just because you're scared he might eat you, you need some kind of secret chamber? That's nuts. You know, if you care about him and he wants to eat you, he should be able to eat you. Get your priorities straight, King." There was a sound of teeth on ligament, like the snapping of chewing gum. She turned to Ira. "Ow. Stop."

She turned back to Max.

"Did that offend you, Max? I'm sorry if you were offended by that. You know, people don't always like me because I say what's on my mind. I tell the truth, but I do it for the good of everyone. And the truth is, if this little secret door maneuver of yours does what I think it'll do, someone else might see fit to eat you. I might have to eat you myself."

"No, no, no!" a voice was yelling from the fort.

It was Carol. He was on his knees, his ear to the ground. "Wait wait wait. What's that? That's not right."

Douglas was close by. "What is it?"

"It's bad," Carol whispered.

"Is it chatter?" Douglas asked.

"So much chatter," Carol said.

Judith and Ira rushed over.

"And what about the whispering?" Judith asked.

"Yup. There's a lot of whispering," Carol said, lifting his head and looking to all of them gravely. "I'm afraid it's reached us here, even inside these high walls."

Alexander was hyperventilating. "What does that mean? We won't be safe here?"

"I'm not sure," Carol said. "But I do know that something's wrong with the design of this fort." He turned to look at Max. "Something's very wrong. I *knew* there shouldn't be secret doors. Arrrgh!"

Carol stormed around the walls. He glared at the secret doors with unchecked contempt.

Now Max was on his knees, listening for whatever it was that Carol heard. Max couldn't hear anything.

"There can't be chatter here," Max said. "Not inside the fort. It's too big and powerful to worry about things like that."

Carol gave him a look registering disappointment in a dozen varieties. He began to mark walls and beams with his claws. "We'll have to start over," he said.

"But the fort's not done yet," Max said. "Shouldn't we wait— "

Carol cut him off. "Max. Your voice is one I don't want to hear right now. We need to remake it. We need to tear down all these parts and start over. We'll need a moat. And higher walls. And an outer wall. I don't know what I was thinking. It could never have made us safe, the way it was designed."

A black mood passed over everyone.

Night came and Max was afraid. The beasts were acting strangely. Alexander was crying so hard he was hiccuping. Judith was off in a corner, eating tiny cats by the handful, while Ira gnawed on her leg.

"Max, come to me," Katherine said.

She was in a quiet and dark corner of the fort. Max went to her, letting her close her arms around him. But just as Max was beginning to feel safe and was drifting off to sleep, he looked out and saw that Carol was staring intently at the two of them together. Carol's eyes narrowed and he returned to clawing at the walls of the fort, marking it for destruction.

CHAPTER XLIII

Carol's voice boomed through the darkness.

"Wake up! Wake up! Get out here! Everybody come out here! Now!"

Everyone woke up, disoriented, and walked outside. It was the middle of the night. Carol was staring into the sky.

"Look!" he roared. "What are we going to do?"

"What's wrong?" Douglas asked.

"Where is it? It's supposed to be right there!" Carol roared.

"What?" Douglas asked.

"The sun! The sun hasn't come up!" Carol said.

Everyone else was hanging back, thinking it better that Douglas handle the problem.

"What do you mean, Carol?" he asked measuredly. "I... Well, I think it's still night."

"No it's not," Carol said gravely. "I didn't sleep. I've been up all night, counting the hours. It's morning, Douglas."

Ira gasped.

"But it's dark," Ira noted.

"*Exactly*," Carol said, pointing to Ira as if he were the only sane one among them.

Now Douglas looked to the sky as if beginning to see Carol's point. "Maybe it's just late to come up," he said.

"Don't be an idiot," Carol fumed. "It's never late!" And now he looked at Max. "It's dead!"

Max tried to protest. "No! That's not gonna happen for a long time."

Judith turned to Max. "What do you mean? How do you know?"

"I told him— "

"You told him the sun was gonna die?" Judith said, enraged. "What did I tell you about saying things to upset Carol? And why didn't you tell *us*?"

Alexander ran to Judith and hid between her legs. "The sun can't die, can it?"

"Of course it can," Carol said. "And it just did!"

Ira's hands were over his mouth. "Oh my god. The void. It's really here."

All of the beasts stared at the place in the sky where the sun was supposed to be. There was nothing but black.

Now Max was worried. Though he knew in his heart that the sun would not, could not, die for millions of years, he was starting to believe that Carol might be right, that the sun had indeed died just hours ago. Maybe things were different on this island.

"We have to think of a new way to live," Carol said. "And the first thing we do is get rid of this fort."

252

"What?" Max said.

Carol ignored him. "Douglas, start tearing it down."

"What's wrong with it?" Douglas asked.

"Everything!" Carol said, and kicked down one of the interior walls. "This fort was designed so that things like this wouldn't happen. And now they've happened. It's a failure, and I want it taken down completely."

"Please," Douglas said. "Not again. Just wait— "

Carol kicked down another wall. "Wait for what? Another sun to grow in the sky? This fort is just a reminder of our failures."

"Carol, calm down," Douglas said, putting his hand on Carol's shoulder.

Carol shook himself free. "Don't try to calm me. This is the end of the world, and you're trying to be calm? I knew I couldn't trust you."

Carol ran himself into one of the log-pillars holding up the roof. It cracked and sent half of the ceiling crashing to the ground. It barely missed Alexander, who began to cry and shudder.

"There you go again," Douglas said.

Carol ignored him and turned to the other beasts.

"We need to take this fort down. Let's go. Right now. No one will be safe in there."

"Yeah, not with you around," Douglas said, blocking his path.

Carol followed him, exploding. "What does *that* mean? *I'm* dangerous? *I'm* scary? Ira, tear it down!"

Douglas wheeled on him. "Fine, you're going to tear it down eventually anyway. Burn everything!"

"Shut up!" Carol yelled.

"Eat everyone!" Douglas hissed.

"Maybe I will!" Carol yelled, and grabbed Douglas's arm, as if to pull him away. But Carol intended something else, and succeeded: he pulled Douglas's arm off. He ripped it from the socket and held it aloft, as if he'd grabbed something rotten and rank.

Douglas stood with wet sand pouring from his shoulder. He put pressure on the hole with his other hand, but the sand leaked between his feathered fingers.

"Your arm's not so great now, is it, Douglas?" Carol said, and tossed it away like it was nothing.

Douglas stalked off, and Katherine followed him, trying to stanch the sand from flowing. Max was left standing in the doorway to the fort, and there he locked eyes with Carol. Carol looked afraid, knowing he could never take back what he'd just done and what Max had just seen. He turned away and walked into the woods.

Just then, the first light of day split the darkness like a knife prying the sky from the earth. The white gumdrop sun broke the horizon and the birds began to gossip from the trees.

CHAPTER XLIV

Max entered the remains of the fort, with Judith, Ira, the Bull, and Alexander close behind.

"So wait," Alexander said, "the sun's not dead? That's the same one?"

"Yes it's the same sun," Judith snapped, looking intensely at Max. "It was just *nighttime*!" She stormed up to Max. "Things sure have gotten messed up since you got here. We just got scared out of our minds because *you* made Carol think the sun was going to die!"

Alexander, hiding behind Judith, added his own invective: "Douglas lost his arm because you needed a fort," he said. "It was a bad idea."

"I know that!" Max said.

"Well, you have a lot of bad ideas!" Judith said.

"I KNOW!" he said.

Judith loomed over him. "I'm hungry. Aren't you, Ira?"

Ira, even Ira, had narrow eyes for Max. "Kind of. Yeah."

"No you're not," Max said, standing his ground. "No one's hungry."

Judith looked at him as if he were a grape who had learned to speak. "Who says?"

"I do. I'm the king."

Alexander scoffed. "King? You're just a boy pretending to be a wolf pretending to be a king."

Max glared at Alexander. He'd never hated a face more than he hated Alexander's. "I'm not pretending to be the king!"

Alexander rolled his eyes. "Then you're just not a very good one."

"Yes I am!" Max yelled.

"You don't even know who you are!"

Max lunged. He tackled Alexander against the fort wall. Alexander hit his head hard and fell to the floor. Max leaped on top of him and began beating him with his fists. He'd never hit anyone so hard and so many times. It felt so good, his knuckles against Alexander's scratchy face, Alexander's arms flailing to block the blows. Max punched and punched until his arms were tired and his knuckles were sore. He punched until Alexander had stopped shrieking and crying and was curled tight, waiting for it to end.

When Max finished and rose to his feet, the beasts were staring at him with what seemed to be a new respect.

"I kinda liked that," Judith said, then burst into a quick trill of a laugh.

"Me too," Ira said.

Max was dazed. He couldn't look at the beasts. He didn't want to be near them or anyone. He needed to be away from them and everyone for a while. If he could leave his own skin, he would have.

He left the fort and wandered toward the sun, which was hovering low over the water like a mother over her children.

CHAPTER XLV

Max spent a few hours at the beach, thinking about what he could and couldn't do, and what he had to do. The sun was high when he made his way back to the fort.

He found the beasts curled up in various parts of the half-ruined fort, napping after their sleepless night. Douglas was there, his head on Judith's stomach, and Ira's arm was hanging over Douglas's, as if protecting the wound from being known. The Bull was asleep, his back flat on the ground and his limbs splayed in surrender.

Max saw another figure in a far dark corner of the fort. He walked closer to find Alexander sitting inside the king's chamber, behind the secret door, left ajar.

Max sat down outside the door.

"You want me to move?" Alexander whispered.

"No," Max said. He looked closely at Alexander, realizing at last that they were more alike than different. Their size, their fur — they were versions of the same undersized and overtrying creature. He thought about putting his hand on Alexander's back, but when he raised his arm, Alexander flinched. There was a raw wound there, the fur missing and the skin red and bruised.

"Did I do that?" Max said.

"Yeah."

Max stared at the wound for a moment, then knelt down next to Alexander.

"Does it hurt?" Max asked, hoping the answer was no.

"A little, yeah," Alexander said, wincing.

Max took the tail of his wolf suit in his hand and licked it, using it to clean the wound.

Alexander smiled. "That's better. Thanks."

"I have to leave and go somewhere else now."

"Where?" Alexander asked.

"Anywhere. I ruin every place I go. I ruined this place, too. I... I didn't want Douglas's arm to... to get..."

Max couldn't say it.

"You didn't rip it off," Alexander said. "Carol did."

"But I wanted a fort. And I told Carol the sun would die. And I wanted secret doors..."

Alexander looked at Max like he was mad. "You really think you wrecked this island? You think you're that powerful? That you're the reason that everyone is happy or sad?"

Max wanted to say *No*, but this is exactly what he was thinking. "But I hit you. I hit you a hundred times."

"Well, you did do that. No doubt about it."

Max finished cleaning the wound and dropped his tail.

"That's why I need to leave. I don't want to ever do anything like that again."

"But you still might," Alexander said.

"But I don't want to."

"But you still might. Wherever you go."

Max wasn't sure if he was making himself clear.

"But I don't *want* to," he said.

Alexander barely paused. Instead, he smiled, as if Max was being particularly dense.

"But you still might."

They sat in silence for a while, watching the rest of the beasts sleeping. In their slumber, the giant creatures were infant-like, almost cute, and at the same time pathetic, tragic, burdened by all they carried with them, far more than Max or Alexander could know.

"With all they've done, all they've devoured, all they've said and— " Alexander laughed.

"What?" Max said. "What do you mean?"

"Well, it's amazing they sleep at all," Alexander said.

CHAPTER XLVI

Max needed to see Carol. He could only think of one place he'd be, now that he knew the sun would live another day.

Max ran across the island, through the forests and over the lava field and to the rocks along the shore. He could see Carol's studio up high above the cliffs, but there were no boulders there to climb on. Max and Carol had thrown them all into the sea below.

Max went back into the lava field and approached the studio from above. It was more difficult than the boulder route, and he felt terrible about having made it harder to get there. He would apologize for that, and a good deal more, when he saw Carol.

When he entered the studio, Carol wasn't there. But he'd been there recently. The entire mini-city had been ravaged. There were remnants of it splayed out, glass and metal everywhere, as if Carol had destroyed it in a rage.

Fish lay all over the floor, one or two still breathing slowly, and at that moment Max realized that Carol had actually gone through with his ideas, building Max's underwater city, complete with a submarine subway train. Max felt sick seeing all of Carol's work crushed and splintered.

He knew he had to find Carol. He turned and ran back over the lava field and through the forest, in the direction of the fort. But when he got close, he saw a dark spiral of smoke coming from the site. He ran faster, and when he came to the edge of the quarry, where he'd stood with Carol to survey the progress, he could see that the fort was on fire, engulfed, all of it orange and trembling. The fort stood no chance of survival. Above, the owls circled and cawed loudly.

"Is that what you wanted?" It was Carol. He had stepped out in front of Max. His face was a cloud of anger, his fur taking the orange of the bonfire behind him.

Max backed up. "No," he said. "I didn't want that. How did it happen?"

Carol shrugged theatrically. "Who knows? Maybe I know, but maybe I won't tell. Just like you didn't tell me you were leaving this island. Are you really going?"

Max nodded.

Carol's face went soft. "Don't," he said quietly.

"I have to," Max said.

Carol turned around quickly, as if stifling an urge to lunge at Max. He turned back to Max, straining to appear genial. "Okay," he said, "but will you come over here and put your head in my mouth again?"

Max continued to back up. "No, Carol. I don't want

to right now." He was intent on creating more space between himself and Carol.

Carol breathed intensely through his nostrils. His face twisted into a pinch. A growl came from deep within. He composed himself and said, evenly, "You're a failure as a king, Max."

Carol stepped toward him, baring his teeth. "Look at your fort, ruined, on fire! Is that what you wanted? Look what you've done!"

Max stood his ground. "I didn't burn the fort down."

"What, you think it's *my* fault? It's *my* fault that you're hurtful?" Carol's eyes were wild. "It's *my* fault that this place is torn apart?"

Max said nothing. He took a few steps back. Carol matched each of Max's backward steps with one forward stride.

"Answer me!" he yelled.

"It's not *my* fault," Max said, and flinched.

"What, it's *my* fault that you beat Alexander? It's *my* fault that you're leaving? That you don't feel safe here? Am I *that* bad? Am I really that *terrible*? Is it *my* fault *your kingdom* is a *failure*?"

Max plotted an escape. He looked left and right.

"Is it *my* fault that I have to eat you?" Carol roared, raising his arms. His claws glowed in the firelight.

Max turned to run.

Carol lunged. Max dropped to all fours. Carol missed. Max rolled off the path and scampered off into the woods. He darted through a low, small opening in the dense thicket — too small for Carol to fit through — and now he had a head start. Max ran through the winding woods, Carol's roaring and heavy footsteps close behind. As he ran, Max had to jump over logs and rocks and duck under low boughs, while he could hear Carol, just behind him, simply steamrolling through it all. Max could hear his breathing, raw and rasping. He was gaining ground.

"Come here!" said a voice, not Carol's.

It was Katherine, standing in the hollow of a tree. She grabbed Max's arm and yanked him off the path. She threw him on her back and scampered up the tree.

Carol ran by, growling ferociously. There was nothing left of the former Carol. He was only rage now, all heat and snarl, with the dull and murderous eyes of a shark.

Katherine reached the top of the tree in seconds and Max looked around, at the hills and shores of the island. He felt safe for a moment, but then the tree began shaking. Carol was climbing up, following them.

"Get inside!" Katherine whispered.

"What?"

Katherine had her mouth open, and was trying to shove Max inside.

"Get in!"

"I don't— "

The shaking grew more violent as Carol grew closer. Max had no choice. He put his arms inside Katherine's mouth, not unlike he'd done when helping Carol the first night. Immediately Katherine shoved Max the rest of the way in, swallowing him. Max let out a quick squeal and was gone, inside Katherine's soft stomach.

It was like being dropped into a cloth bag full of wet

food. The smell was musty and ripe, a mixture of rotten food and stomach acid. It was dark and stifling, with only the occasional gasp of air or light when Katherine opened her mouth.

Carol thundered close and soon he was on the platform, too, hovering over Katherine. Max felt her leaning back, trying to retain her balance.

"Where is he?" he roared.

Max tried to breathe as quietly as possible.

"Where's who?" Katherine said.

"Don't make this worse," Carol bellowed, now even louder. "Where is he, Katherine?"

"I don't know!" she shouted, defiant.

"You want me to eat *you*, too?"

"Go ahead!" she yelled.

Carol shoved her and, with a massive shaking of the platform, Max could tell that Carol had leapt off. But just as Max began to feel relief, there was an explosion of movement and screaming. Carol was back, and the platform creaked and groaned from the strain.

"Give him to me!" Carol yelled.

"He's not here!" Katherine said, her teeth gritted.

"Wait," he hissed. "I *smell* him."

Max could hear Carol just outside the thin wall of skin and fur that separated the two of them.

"I can smell him on your breath!"

Carol's huge claw plunged into Katherine's stomach, grabbing for Max. Max dodged Carol's paw, jostling around inside Katherine's belly. Max felt something tense up inside Katherine and suddenly, with a deep grunt of pain, Carol's hand was gone. Katherine had struck him, it seemed, with all her force, and he'd fallen from the top of the tree, easily two hundred feet down. Max could hear the cracking of branches as Carol descended, trying to break his fall. Finally there was a thump, and a low groan.

"Hold on," Katherine said to Max, and he felt her leap from the platform and to another. Then another. She jumped high and away, again and again, until Max was sure they had found their way across the island and to safety.

CHAPTER XLVII

When they were still, Max could smell, faintly, the salt water of the sea. Katherine, with Max in her belly, had escaped all the way to her beach. He was relieved and tired and wanted only to get out and to sail away.

"Is he gone?" Max asked.

"He is," Katherine said. "We're safe."

Max was dazed and short of breath. "I can't breathe that well in here. Can you get me out?"

Katherine said nothing.

"Katherine?" Max said, louder.

There was no answer.

"Katherine!" he yelled, now pounding on the wall of her stomach.

He began to try to climb the walls of Katherine's insides, but they were far too slippery. There was nothing to grab onto.

"Katherine?" he asked.

Finally she answered. "What is it, my darling?"

"What are you doing? I need to get out."

Max heard nothing.

"Katherine?"

There was no response.

"Katherine? Where are you?"

"You're safe inside," she said. "I'll protect you."

"What?" Max said.

"Don't you like it in there?" she asked.

"No. Let me out."

There was another long pause before she spoke again.

"You were a bad king. I can't let you go."

"What? I was not a bad king. Katherine, I need to get out." Max was short of breath and his head was pulsating. "I don't think I'm supposed to be in here. I can't breathe."

"Yes you can," she insisted. "Why are you doing this to me?" she asked, suddenly outraged. "You don't love me!"

"That's not true," Max said. "Why would you say that?"

"I don't know!" she wailed.

Max was growing weaker inside, his breathing shallower. He felt very faint.

"Please don't go, Max. You're a part of me."

"I have to go," he whispered.

There was a pause that seemed interminable. Max found himself growing numb, his fingers tingling, his heart fluttering.

Just as he felt himself dropping into something like sleep, he was lifted toward the light. It was Katherine. She had thrust her arm into her mouth, taking hold of Max by the scruff of his neck. She lifted Max from her stomach and into the air, and carefully deposited him on her lap.

The air felt so cold and clean, and he gulped at it. The ocean beyond them was bright and calm, and pulled at Max. But he felt so weak that he couldn't keep his eyes open. As Katherine stroked his wet hair, he dropped into a shallow sleep.

CHAPTER XLVIII

When he awoke he saw all of the beasts, all but Carol, before him. They had untied his boat and had prepared it to sail. Max rose from Katherine's lap and stood, still feeling light-headed.

"So you're going," Douglas said. His leg, half-eaten by the plant, was green and smelled like ham. There was a stick tied to his shoulder, in place of his missing arm.

Max nodded.

Douglas extended his left hand. Max shook it.

"You were the best thinker we ever had," Douglas said.

Max tried to smile.

"I'm sorry for all this," Ira said quietly. "I blame myself."

Max hugged him. "Don't."

Judith and Max exchanged glances. She made a face that said *Oops, sorry!* then emitted a high nervous laugh. "I never know what to say in these situations," she said.

Max and Katherine pushed the boat toward the water, and Douglas helped. Max remembered that he was still wearing the crown, and so removed it with great care and presented it to the Bull.

Max's head felt lighter now, his thoughts clearer. Looking at the beasts, he tried to commit each of them to memory. He wished Carol were there, but at the same time he knew that goodbyes were seldom as tidy and timely as one would hope. He turned toward his boat and the sea beyond, squinting to the waves to see what challenges they would present to him.

When the hull had left the sand and was floating in the calm water, Max stepped in. Standing on the stern, he turned to hug Katherine. Her body shook, crying, but when they parted she seemed good, seemed strong.

Max raised his sail and grabbed the rudder. He was ready. Douglas and Ira pushed the boat the last few feet until it was free of the beach.

As the tide took Max out, there was a great rustling through the forest. They all looked up. A pair of great fronds parted and there he was. It was Carol. He broke through the foliage and ran toward the shore, his arms flailing.

Max locked eyes with him and when he did, Carol stooped at the top of the dunes, his shoulders slack. In Carol's face, Max saw only sadness. There was no more anger, no more want, nothing but sorrow and regret.

As the sail pulled Max further away, he and Carol kept their eyes fixed on each other. Almost in a trance, Carol began to walk toward the shore. He descended the dunes and staggered across the beach, his eyes growing more anxious as he approached the sea. He walked past the other beasts and stumbled into the ocean, having no sense of where he was. It wasn't until he was chest-deep in the water that he realized Max was too far away to reach. At that moment Carol looked like he might fall apart, dropping limb by limb into the sea.

Knowing it was the only thing to do, Max howled.

The howl sounded like forgiveness, and this was all, it seemed, Carol wanted. He was overcome, his eyes a mess of tears. He stopped, chest-deep in the ocean, just short of drowning. Gathering himself, he howled in return. "Arooooooo! Arrrroooooooooooooooooooo!"

Their howls rose to the sky and twisted together until they were one, and the other beasts joined in too, all of their voices creating a wild, plaintive song of sorrow and abandon and anger and love. They howled together until Max was far into the sea, gone forever.

CHAPTER XLIX

Max sailed under a full moon, with no land in front of him or behind him. He set his compass south, hoping that traveling in the opposite direction would bring him home. But for all he knew, it might bring him to another land altogether.

He sailed in and out of days and nights, through storms and bright dull mornings so long he thought they'd never cede the afternoon. And finally, one morning, he saw a caterpillar inching across the horizon, and that caterpillar soon grew to become land stretching west and east, and that land grew to become, he was sure, the forest from which he'd pushed off.

When he finally made land, he docked the boat in the same inlet and tied it to the same tree where he'd found it. He ran, as fast as he could, through the forest. The snow had melted and now there were only a few pockets of white. He was so close to home.

He left the forest and reached the road, loving the feel of pavement on his feet. He ran through the neighborhood, all of the houses dark but his own. He could see it clearly in the distance, and from its windows light still shone brightly.

Max ran his fastest until he was a few houses away, when he slowed down to a jog, then a walk. Why did he slow down? It confused Max, too. Perhaps it was the very weight of being home again. He'd been gone so long. Years, it seemed. And now he was back, and he was different. Would his mother recognize him? Would Claire? In some ways he felt too big for this house. But he also felt newly able to fit within it.

Max entered, trying not to make any noise as he closed the door. He passed through the front hallway and saw his art-class bird, which had miraculously been repaired. Upon closer inspection he could see that his mother had fixed it, with the utmost delicacy and care. It was whole and new again.

Passing through the kitchen, Max saw on the counter a whole meal laid out for him — a bowl of cream of mushroom soup, a glass of milk, and a slice of cake. Still standing, he ate with greedy gulps, and while doing so he saw his mom, asleep on the couch.

He swallowed the food, slipped the wolf hood off his head, and walked to her. Standing over her, Max could see that she had fallen asleep with her glasses on. Her hair was matted close to her temple.

Max stared down at her, his head tilted, watching her. He carefully removed her glasses and set them silently on the table before her. He touched her face gently, pushing a strand of hair back behind her ear. He stood above his mother for some time, knowing her now, really almost knowing her now, happy to watch her rest.

ACKNOWLEDGMENTS

It goes without saying that this book would not exist without Maurice Sendak and Spike Jonze. Back in 1963, Maurice published a strange and unprecedented picture book, a book I read as a child, was terrified by, and finally came to grips with somewhere in my early twenties. Epochs later, Spike called me out of the blue one day in 2003, asking me if I'd like to collaborate on the screenplay for a film adaptation he was doing of the book. I said yes, and I owe him an incalculable amount for thinking of me, and not, say, an experienced screenwriter.

And so the process began. Spike laid out the basics of what he had in mind — that Max was the son of divorced and somewhat distracted parents, that he had a sister, and that when he sails to the island, the journey, and the island, and all those he meets there, are very real. Spike and I tried to flesh out the story from there, starting with the question of not *where* but *who* the Wild Things are, and what they want from life and from Max.

Over the years (decades?) we worked on the script, I was able to meet Mr. Sendak, as true and uncompromising an artist and genuine a man as there ever was. Maurice called one day and said that the idea had occurred to him and others that a novel could be written from all this accumulated material, and he asked if I'd like to do it. I said I would try, and this is the result.

If you've seen the movie, you will notice that the story here hews closely to the movie in many places, and departs in others. When sitting down to write this book, I thought at first that I would more or less transcribe the movie. But along the way, while getting lost, Max-like, in the thicket of the plot, I found other pathways into and out of the island, and generally added my own interpretations to the story of Max. The children's-book Max is, after all, a version of Maurice, and the movie Max is a version of Spike. The Max of this book, then, is some combination of Maurice's Max, Spike's Max, and the Max of my own boyhood.

For their clear and passionate readings of this book, thanks go to my wife Vendela and brother Toph, both of whom understand the Maxes of the world and thus boyhood, and thus childhood, and thus humanhood; my friends Michelle Quint and Tish Scola and Adrienne Mahar for early and astute reads of the manuscript; Nicholas Thomson, Onnesha Roychoudhuri, and Henry Jones for expert late-game proofing; Vince, Natalie, Russell, KK, Eric, Sonny, John, Ren, both Catherines, and all the other lunatic-genius makers of the film; all the editors and staff at McSweeney's; Daniel and Michael and Nick and Roddy and Neil for leading the way and setting the (high) bar; Simon Prosser, Andrew Wylie, Sally Wilcox, and Deb Klein, who together championed this book at a crucial time; and Mac Barnett, a great young writer of books for young people. If you haven't read his work, run somewhere and do that. Books for young people have a rich and I daresay limitless future — knock anyone who says otherwise into a ditch — and Mac has a central place within that limitless future. Don't bet against him, or anyone like him.